Mallory didn't know dragon shifters existed, and now he wishes he'd never found out. The local dragon clan wants to take out the wolf pack, including Mallory's friends, and he can't let that happen. No one on their team will, and Mallory isn't surprised when they all decide to follow his lead when he announces he's taking a sabbatical from the conclave they work for.

They're staying with the pack, but not everyone is happy about that.

Arlen and his best friend left the clan a long time ago, but he's always known they would never truly be free. He's not surprised when the clan continues selling drugs in his club, and when trying to talk to the clan leader doesn't help.

The clan won't stop until they get what they want.

Arlen didn't expect to meet a vampire and fall for him, but when the club burns down, Mallory is there for him, along with his friends and family. It's something Arlen never had beyond Merrick, and he can't regret any of it, even though he lost the club.

But the clan isn't done with Arlen or with the pack. Can a bunch of vampires, two dragon shifters, and a recalcitrant pack win against them?

Burning Fangs
Copyright © 2022 Catherine Lievens
ISBN: 978-1-4874-3700-8
Cover art by Angela Waters

Published by eXtasy Books Inc

Look for us online at:
www.eXtasybooks.com

Burning Fangs
Life with Fangs 9

By

Catherine Lievens

CHAPTER ONE

This wasn't how Mallory had expected to spend more time with Baxter. He supposed it was better than nothing, but having to deal with a deadly drug first, then, apparently, a clan of dragons who wanted to kill all of them, wasn't great. At least for now, the dragons seemed to have taken a step back.

"You're happy here?" he asked Baxter as they walked in the forest.

Baxter gave him a happy smile. "Very much so."

"Who would have thought? I thought you'd be an enforcer for much longer." Although he could see the appeal of the forest. The night was dark, and the silence was almost too much to be comfortable.

Baxter shrugged. "I never really loved it, not like some enforcers do. I did it because it gave me something to do and because it meant I could spend time with my family."

"And now, you have a new family."

Baxter grinned again. He'd always been a happy person, but it was as if he couldn't stop smiling since he'd met Sloan. Sloan made him happy, and while Mallory hadn't expected any of this, he couldn't say he felt sorry for Baxter.

Or for Robin. What was happening to his team members? He was one of the few who didn't have anyone in his life by now, and at least two of them were leaving the team.

That was one thing Mallory wasn't happy about. He didn't berate Robin and Baxter for wanting to stay with their wolves, but did they have to be so far away? Mallory couldn't help but wonder who would replace them, and it wasn't something he was comfortable with. They were more than a team. They'd been together for so long that they were a family, and losing two people, then adding another two they didn't know, wasn't going to be easy. It made him wonder if maybe he should leave the team, too, but then the members who didn't would be stuck there, having lost him, too. What would that help?

"So when are you going back?" Baxter asked.

"Going back? We're not going anywhere until this thing with the dragons is solved."

"Yeah? That's good to hear, because I don't think the pack is ready to take on a dragon clan. I mean, they didn't even know the dragons were so close or that they existed."

"I don't blame them for that. I wasn't aware dragons existed, either. For animals so big, they sure can hide."

"But I'm worried. What if they decide to attack the pack? I'll do everything to protect the wolves, and I know I'm not the only one, but these guys are *dragons*."

"I'm sure we'll find a way to deal with this."

"I do feel better knowing the team is staying."

"I don't know about the team, but I know I am. I doubt any of them would want to leave you alone with dragons around." But Baxter's question had made Mallory wonder. He needed to talk to Oren and find out what they were supposed to do next. The conclave was the one who gave orders, after all. They couldn't just decide they wanted to stay.

"I'll miss all of you," Baxter murmured. He kicked the root of one of the trees they walked past. He looked more surly now, almost like a child.

"Well, I know we don't stand a chance next to your Sloan."

"I wouldn't be staying here if it weren't for him."

"I know. You're in love."

Baxter sighed, as if that was a problem. "I never expected

any of this. I thought I'd stay with the team for a long time, and I'm not sure I'm ready to let you guys go."

Mallory reached out and squeezed Baxter's arm. Baxter's pale cheeks were flushed, and his red hair flopped in front of his eyes. He needed a haircut, but maybe he wouldn't get one. If he wasn't going to fight with the team, it wasn't essential for him to be able to see without hindrance, was it? He didn't have to follow the conclave's orders anymore, even when it came to his hair or his clothes.

"You're not letting us go," he said. "No matter what happens and where we end up, you'll still be part of our team. You're part of our *family*, and that's all that matters. Just because you're not with us doesn't change that."

"It's just going to be weird, you know? I haven't been with the team for long, but it's still hard to make this decision."

"Fighting was never for you." Mallory knew that Baxter had never been interested in being an enforcer. It had been something to pass the time, which, when you were a vampire, you had plenty of. Baxter disliked fighting and following orders, and it was a good thing that he could finally leave the conclave behind. Mallory suspected that he hadn't left sooner because he didn't want to lose their family.

They stopped in front of the house Baxter now shared with Sloan. They faced each other, with Baxter nervously shuffling his feet.

"We're not leaving yet," Mallory told him. "You're not going to get rid of us so easily, so stop worrying."

Baxter nodded, then, to Mallory's surprise, threw his arms around him. He squeezed Mallory, and Mallory hugged back. They weren't usually touchy-feely with the team members, but that didn't mean they didn't care about each other. Baxter clearly needed this, and Mallory was more than happy to oblige.

"Your wolf will be jealous if he sees us," Mallory said with a chuckle.

"He's not like that. He knows how much you guys matter to me."

"I know. I was joking."

They took a step away from each other. Baxter's cheeks looked like they were on fire, but that didn't stop him from grinning. "I'm glad to have all of you here."

"And we're glad to be here. These wolves are your and Robin's family now, which means we'll protect them with all we have."

"Even though some of them wish you weren't here?"

Mallory was pretty sure some of them wished they could kill the entire team, but he didn't say that out loud. If Baxter didn't already know how angry and opposed to his presence some of the pack members were, he'd find out soon enough. He could defend himself, and besides, Sloan wouldn't allow anyone to mistreat him. Baxter knew that sometimes life wasn't easy and that not everyone would like him. Unfortunately, it had more to do with *what* he was than with the person he was, but there were idiots everywhere.

"We're used to dealing with people who don't want us, aren't we? This isn't any different from other missions we were on."

"I promise no one here will try to kill you." Baxter wrinkled his nose. "Well, apart from dragons. I'm pretty sure they're going to try to kill everyone."

"And we'll face them if they try." Mallory didn't want to talk about this anymore. The night was warm, the moon high in the sky, and they weren't on a mission for once. "I'll see you soon?"

That brought the smile back to Baxter's face. "Just give me time to grab a shower and some clothes. I'll come around and pick you up."

"I'll be waiting."

They were going to the club owned by the dragon. Mallory still wasn't sure they could trust him, but maybe tonight could be as much about fun as be about observing the dragons and finding out if they truly weren't working with their clan. Mallory hadn't been there when Baxter and the others had talked to the dragon shifter, but Baxter had told the team about it, and Mallory was curious. It would also be good to have a dragon on their side rather than on the clan's side. If they wanted to kick dragon ass, they needed to know where to find that ass and how to do it.

He walked back to the house he and the rest of the team shared. He crossed paths with a wolf in their wolf form, and while they snarled at him, they stayed away. That was good, because Mallory didn't fancy getting into a fight with a wolf, and not just because of the wolf's fangs. How would it look if he started fighting with the people Robin and Baxter now lived with?

His phone vibrated in his pocket, and he took it out to see his brother's name on the screen. He wanted to talk to Alpin, but he heard Oren's voice coming from the living room as he reached the house. It didn't sound good, so he just shot a quick text to his brother and made his way toward Oren.

The living room door was closed. Oren didn't usually make a secret of his phone calls with the conclave, and he always said that since he was going to have to order them anyway, they might as well hear it from the source, but today had to be different. Today, the door was closed, and Mallory worried.

Arlen was going over the accounts when someone knocked on his office door. He could have kissed whoever was there, distracting him from all the money he was spending for the club.

At least he was also earning money.

He let go of his computer mouse and leaned back in his chair. "Come in," he called out.

The door opened, and Merrick stepped in. Arlen was always happy to see his fellow dragon shifter, but usually Merrick's appearance in his office during the evening meant something was happening in the club. It wasn't good most of the time, so Arlen tensed and got ready to hear whatever was wrong now.

"There's a group of vampires in the club," Merrick said. His light brown hair was swept away from his face, and like always, his expression was unforgiving.

If Arlen hadn't known him as well as he did, he might have been intimidated. But they'd grown up together, and he knew Merrick almost better than he knew himself. Merrick could defend himself and the club if he had to, but he wasn't one to start a fight just because he felt like it.

"And we're worried about them?" he asked.

Merrick shrugged. "I don't know about you. I'm certainly worried."

"Why? Are they doing something that worries you?"

"They're from the pack."

Arlen rubbed his forehead. The pack and the people who came with it were complications he hadn't expected. He wasn't sure what to do with them, but he wouldn't allow his old clan to hurt anyone, not even wolves. He didn't particularly want to fight his clan, but he also couldn't stand by and watch them give deadly drugs to vampires and wolves. At least the vampires had found out what the dragons were doing, and they knew to be careful.

"Are they doing something they shouldn't be doing?" he asked.

"Not that I could see."

"Then maybe you should stop worrying about them."

Merrick narrowed his eyes. "And how am I supposed to do that? You know what's going on between them and the clan."

Arlen did. He'd saved one of the vampires when an old employee had tried drugging him. Well, the situation had been more complicated than that, but in the end, it meant he'd met the vampire and the wolves he lived with.

That was an odd mix, but it worked, from what Arlen had seen. Besides, it wouldn't be the first time vampires mixed with other supernatural creatures. He'd seen many things in his long life, and when people lived as long as he and vampires did, they tended not to care about what people were for long. Well, either that or they cared too much and became extremists.

He got to his feet. "I'll go say hello."

Merrick frowned. "That's not why I came to tell you about them. I just wanted you to be aware of what was happening."

Arlen waved his words away and moved toward the tiny private bathroom at the back of his office. He checked his reflection in the mirror, leaving the door open so he could hear Merrick talking. "Why shouldn't I say hello?"

"I never said you shouldn't. I'm just not sure it's a good idea."

"Well, the club is still mine, the last time I checked."

Merrick crossed his arms over his chest and arched a brow. "Is it, now?"

Merrick had been next to him, helping him financially and in any way he could, as Arlen built the club and opened it. They were always teasing each other about it, so Arlen knew Merrick wasn't offended.

"Look, you said they're not doing anything they shouldn't be doing. Why can't I say hello?" he asked as he turned to face his friend.

"Because the clan could be watching."

Arlen sighed. "They're always watching. We knew what

would happen when we left the clan, and I know you're not surprised about any of this."

"Not surprised, but worried."

Arlen left the bathroom and stopped next to Merrick. "I'll be fine. Besides, the clan has been looking for a reason to attack us for years. They might use the vampires, just like they could have used something else. It was only a matter of time, and apparently, they're ready for us."

"This isn't going to end well," Merrick muttered.

The two of them moved toward the office door.

"Maybe, maybe not. Hiding in my office isn't going to solve anything, though. I don't care if the clan finds out I'm talking to the vampires. If not for them, the clan would just find another reason to attack me eventually. Might as well get it out of the way."

"I'll kill you if you get yourself killed," Merrick warned.

Arlen laughed. "Understood. The same goes for you, of course. Try to keep breathing for a while longer."

As soon as Arlen opened his office door, the sounds of the club assaulted him. By now, he was used to the smells and the noise, but when he spent a lot of time in his office, it was still a shock. He gave himself a moment for his senses to get used to it, then walked down the hallway and headed toward the central part of the club.

The floor vibrated under his feet from the music and the many people on the dance floor. The air smelled of too-strong perfume, alcohol, and sweat—a mix Arlen had gotten used to by now. It was good to see so many people dancing and drinking. More than the money, he cared about giving supernatural creatures a place where they could be safe. Most of the people here belonged to supernatural communities, and those who didn't were aware of them. There was no finding Midnight by accident. Arlen had made sure of that, and he'd paid handsomely for it.

"They're at a booth," Merrick said in Arlen's ear.

"You put them there?"

"I thought it would be for the best. Something told me you'd want to see them."

Arlen smiled. Merrick knew him, that was for sure.

He allowed his friend to steer him in the direction where he'd stashed the vampires. Arlen would have been able to find them, but it would have taken him more time, and the less he was seen in the club, the better it was.

When they reached the booth, Arlen recognized a few of the people sitting there. The easiest vamp to remember was the redhead who'd almost been drugged the last time he'd been there. He didn't seem to hold a grudge, but Arlen still gestured at the waiter to come closer to let him know whatever the vampires consumed was on the house.

"You didn't have to do that," Baxter said. He was almost bouncing in his seat.

"It's the least I can do after what happened last time. I hope you're all having fun?"

"I like this place." Baxter pointed at the people at the table whom Arlen didn't know. "This is Gladys, Renata, and Mallory. And you already know Sloan."

Arlen gave the group a slight bow. Sloan looked like he'd rather be anywhere but here, but the vampires appeared curious about Midnight. One of them, the male, caught Arlen's attention.

How could he not? Mallory, as Baxter had called him, was blond, and his brown eyes spoke of gentleness and strength. None of them were wearing uniforms, but from the way they kept an eye on their surroundings and how they sat, Arlen could tell they worked for the vampire conclave.

"I'm Arlen, the owner of this club," he said, smiling. "And this is Merrick. If you need anything, feel free to tell either of us."

"Are you having a drink with us?" Baxter asked.

He had a bubbly personality that Arlen wasn't sure was a good mix with being an enforcer, although considering the way he and Sloan were together, maybe he wouldn't be an enforcer for long.

"He probably has work to do," Mallory said.

He was staring at Arlen, and Arlen stared back. Their gazes caught, and while Mallory's eyes widened — probably when he realized that Arlen's eyes were red — he didn't look away. Arlen wanted to know more about the vampire, so he nodded instead of gracefully declining Baxter's offer like he usually would. "One drink won't take me away from my work for long."

Merrick groaned and muttered something that Arlen didn't catch, but he could imagine what his friend was saying. Dating a vampire was the last thing Arlen needed at the moment.

He didn't care.

Mallory couldn't deny that one of the reasons he'd agreed to come to the club was to meet a dragon shifter. Even after Baxter had described the man to him, he hadn't known what to expect, but it was so much more than he could have imagined.

He'd been startled when his gaze crossed with Arlen's and he'd seen the man's eyes were red. Most supernatural creatures looked human. That made sense, since most of the population was human and they needed to be able to hide in their midst. There was nothing human about Arlen's eyes, though. Mallory hadn't seen them very well, considering the club's darkness and colorful lights, but well enough to know they were red. He couldn't pass that off to humans as an odd eye color.

Baxter squeezed closer to Sloan to give Arlen space on his

side of the table. That placed Arlen in front of Mallory, who was sitting with Renata and Gladys.

Mallory couldn't look away. Arlen swiped a strand of dark hair away from his face, exposing his face. His jaw was square, and his eyes twinkled with something Mallory couldn't identify. His nose was straight, with just a few freckles peppered on the skin. He didn't have nearly as many as Baxter, but Mallory still wanted to count all of them.

Was it bad to be attracted to a dragon shifter when you weren't sure you could trust him?

It wasn't the first time Mallory was attracted to someone inconvenient, but he'd have to work with Arlen. It would have been better to ignore the dragon, but Mallory wasn't sure he could. Arlen seemed to have the same problem, and while it was easy to see how this could end in disaster, Mallory hoped it wouldn't.

"So, you're in town to fight the clan," Arlen said.

The waiter serving Mallory and the others had disappeared, probably to get Arlen a drink. He hadn't had to ask what Arlen wanted, but then, Arlen was his boss. Even though Mallory suspected that Arlen didn't often drink with the partygoers in the club, it was clear his people knew what he liked.

Mallory leaned closer. "We're here to make sure the clan doesn't hurt the pack. As long as they stay away, we won't fight them." Or at least, Mallory thought that was how things would go. The conclave didn't usually start fights when they didn't need to, especially when they couldn't be sure they'd win. The dragons were an unknown quantity, and it wouldn't be easy to find out their strengths and weaknesses. Mallory hoped Arlen would make it easier on them if needed, but he wouldn't be surprised if the dragon didn't. He might not be part of his clan anymore, but they were still his people.

"It's clear you don't know the clan," Arlen said. "They

know what they want, and in this situation, it's to get rid of the pack and as many vampires as possible. They hoped the wolves and the vampires would kill each other, and I have no doubt they're regrouping and coming up with new ideas, but they won't step aside just because they've been defeated once."

Mallory's fingers tightened around his glass. He'd expected an answer like that but had hoped for the opposite. "So you think they'll attack the pack?"

Just then, the waiter appeared, carrying a tray. There was a tall glass on it, with a little paper umbrella. He placed the drink in front of Arlen, who nodded at him in thanks. Arlen waited for the waiter to leave before he started talking again.

"I have no doubt they will. What they want above all is power. It can never be enough for them, and while they could dismiss the pack as long as the alpha's father was still in charge, they can't anymore. The new alpha is different, and he won't stand for some of the things the clan has done the way his father had."

Mallory didn't know much about the situation between Kieran, Sloan, and their father. He did know that their father wasn't the alpha anymore and that not every pack member was happy about that. Mallory knew that Kieran was a much better alpha than his father could ever have been, especially after what Arlen had just said, but maybe it was time to ask a few questions. If he and the team were going to defend the pack, they needed to know everything there was to know about the wolves who lived here.

"So what you're saying is that just like not all wolves are good or bad, the same goes for dragons," Sloan said. "And that we can trust you, even though we can't trust the clan."

"Of course we can trust Arlen," Baxter said. He grabbed Sloan's arm and started to pull. "But since we're here to have fun and not talk about work, why don't you take me on the dance floor?"

Sloan didn't look happy about that, but he didn't say no. Instead, he went along with what Baxter wanted, and Arlen had to get to his feet to let them pass. Mallory expected him to make his excuses since he was up, but instead, he sat back down again.

Gladys elbowed Mallory in the ribs. "Let us up, will you? We want to dance, too."

Mallory obeyed, even though it left him alone with Arlen. The other dragon, Merrick, had disappeared soon after Arlen had sat with them, but Mallory had caught sight of him near the dance floor once.

"You're not going to dance?" Arlen asked.

"I've never been much of a dancer, even though I've had decades to learn. I tend to step on feet when I try to dance."

Arlen chuckled. The sound was light and airy, and it made Mallory want to get even closer. It would be odd if he walked around the table and sat next to Arlen, so he tightened his hand around his drink and stayed where he was.

"I'm not much of a dancer myself," Arlen confessed.

"No? But you're the owner. Why would you want to open a club if you don't dance?"

Arlen took a sip of his drink, clearly trying to find the best way to explain. "When Merrick and I left the clan, we were alone. The clan was all we'd known, and we were lost for a bit. We had more than enough money, so we didn't have to work, but as I'm sure you know, not doing anything gets boring after a while. We were trying to find something to do with our lives when we met two satyrs. Talking with them and getting to know them made us realize that we could be friends even though we belonged to different species. The problem was that often, it's dangerous for different supernatural creatures to mingle in plain sight."

Mallory knew something about that. Vampires never

looked nicely on other supernatural creatures, although they had a particular hate for wolves. Robin and Baxter didn't care about that, nor did the rest of the team, but Mallory had seen enough hate from vampires and wolves to know what Arlen was talking about. He also wasn't surprised to find out that dragon shifters kept to their species, just like vampires did.

"So you decided to open a club where supernatural creatures could mingle?" he asked.

"Exactly. We wanted to facilitate this kind of relationship and give the creatures who already have friends or loved ones who belong to other species a safe place where they could be together. Here, no one will dare say anything about the fact that they don't belong to the same community."

"I like it." Mallory looked around. Although the people dancing were very different from the ones he'd seen in other clubs he visited, the club was a club. There were few humans, and most of the people he could see belonged to a supernatural community.

"I'm glad you do." Arlen's voice was smooth. "And as long as you're in town, you're welcome to visit. You and your entire team are."

"You didn't have anything to do with what the clan has done. You don't have to offer us free drinks to apologize or anything like that."

Arlen stared at Mallory for so long that Mallory felt the need to wiggle in his seat. He didn't, because he'd been trained not to show anyone his weaknesses, but he suspected that Arlen knew how it made him feel. From the way the dragon smiled, Mallory thought he knew many things about him, even though Mallory hadn't told him anything.

"Maybe that's not why I'm offering you free drinks," Arlen said.

"No? Then why are you?" This was dangerous territory, but Mallory didn't care. He was enjoying himself.

Arlen's answering smile held promises Mallory couldn't even begin to wrap his mind around. "Maybe I want to give you an incentive to come back."

Mallory wanted to say he didn't need an incentive to return to the club, but he suspected that Arlen knew that, too.

Arlen could almost hear Merrick's voice in his mind, telling him he was being an idiot. He had no doubt that was what the real Merrick would say, but he didn't care. Mallory might be a complication Arlen didn't need, but it was a complication he wanted.

Arlen had been attracted to many people over the years. He didn't usually date, but he'd had plenty of one-night stands, and that was enough for him. He might just have met Mallory, but he could already tell that one night with the vampire wouldn't be enough—not for him and not for his dragon.

That was the odd part. Usually, the dragon didn't care who Arlen had sex with. If anything, it was a bit annoyed that Arlen gave in to the urges. It was fine taking care of that themselves, but Arlen enjoyed a bit of company. His dragon was awake and interested in Mallory, though, which was enough to tell Arlen that Mallory was a good choice. For whatever reason, Arlen already trusted him. That was more than he could say for most of the people he slept with.

Mallory's cheeks flushed, and he looked away. "I don't need free drinks to come back."

"No? Do you like the club that much then?"

"Not the club. I mean, it's nice and everything, and I like that it's a place where everyone can be themselves without fear of being attacked because of what they are, but clubs aren't really my thing, to be honest."

So it would have been easy for them never to meet. Arlen supposed he had Baxter to thank for this. He'd make sure he did.

"Yet, you said you'd come back."

Mallory shrugged. "All of this is interesting. There aren't many places where you can watch different supernatural creatures interact." His gaze flickered to Arlen. "Or where you can meet dragon shifters. I didn't even know you guys existed until recently."

"We exist, and I'll be more than happy to answer any question you might have about my dragon or me."

And he'd be more than happy to drag Mallory into his office and have his way with him, but he didn't want to risk ruining things. Arlen had no idea where this was going or even if it was going somewhere, but if the clan caught word that he was interested in a vampire, they'd make sure to hurt Mallory to get to Arlen. That wouldn't be enough to keep Arlen away from Mallory, especially since the vampire could clearly defend himself, but he'd have to be honest if things went the way he hoped they would. Mallory would decide whether or not being with Arlen would be worth putting himself into the clan's path.

"That's, ah, good to know. Do you have, you know, a girlfriend? A wife, maybe? Or a boyfriend. It doesn't make a difference. I mean, I don't care either way."

Mallory was so charming, especially when he was flustered. "I have no one important in my life," Arlen said smoothly. "Although if I were to have someone, it would be a male. That's where my preference is." Although most dragons and immortal creatures tended to be all over the rainbow as far as Arlen knew. When one lived as long as they did, they had plenty of time to experiment and experience different kinds of love, both emotional and physical. But Arlen had always leaned more toward men, and he wanted Mallory to know that.

"So Merrick is a friend?"

Ah. Mallory seemed to be jealous, although if he was jealous of Merrick, he shouldn't be. "We've been best friends since we were children. There has been nothing more between us, and there never will be. We don't like each other that way."

Mallory's shoulders relaxed. "Good. Well, I mean, it doesn't matter, but I was curious."

"I completely understand. I don't suppose you're dating one of the ladies here with you tonight?"

"Gosh, no. They're like sisters."

Arlen and his dragon were pleased, but Arlen wasn't sure how to make Mallory see he was interested. He also wasn't sure if the best thing to do was to drag Mallory to his office tonight. Mallory would come back. Arlen didn't doubt that, and when he did come back, things would be different. They were both very much aware of the other and that they found each other attractive, but maybe that was all it was to Mallory. Arlen couldn't dismiss the interest his dragon had in the vampire. It was rare for them to agree on people, which was one more reason to cherish Mallory's presence in his life.

A loud shout made both of them jump. Arlen hadn't even realized they were staring at each other, but now that they weren't, he felt the loss. The sound of a fight breaking out was enough to get him to his feet. It wasn't far from the table where he and Mallory were sitting, and Arlen could feel Mallory's presence next to him as he made his way toward the two people fighting.

He sucked in a breath when he finally reached them and saw who they were. Arlen hadn't forbidden the clan dragons from coming to the club, but they didn't usually. Tonight, though, two were present, and, to no one's surprise, had started the fight. From what Arlen could see, the wolf that the dragon had been fighting with was in one piece, although blood was dripping from his mouth.

"Clement, Warner," he said. "I can't say it's a pleasure to see you here."

Clement, who'd been the one fighting, grinned at him. It wasn't a nice smile, and it wasn't friendly. "We wanted to see what all the fuss was about."

"And you have. You know where the door is."

"What, you're going to kick out two paying customers?"

"I'm kicking out two customers who started a fight. I don't condone violence in my club or out of it."

Clement didn't seem to care what Arlen thought. "How are you going to get us to leave, then? Will you fight us?"

He seemed convinced that he would win, and he just might, but it wouldn't be a good idea to shift in the middle of the club. It was packed, and it would be too easy for Clement to hurt someone if he shifted.

Clement probably didn't care about that.

A movement beside Arlen caught Arlen's attention. He turned to look while still keeping an eye on Clement, and while he wasn't surprised to see Mallory was standing next to him, he wasn't the only one. Merrick was there, glaring at Clement and Warner, but so were Baxter, Sloan, Renata, and Gladys. If Clement and Warner wanted a fight, they'd get one.

"Merrick, can you show Clement and Warner to the door," Arlen asked.

"With pleasure," Merrick said in a hard voice.

"We'll be back," Clement hissed out as he passed by Arlen. "And when we are, you won't be able to kick us out as easily as you are tonight."

Arlen kept a smile plastered on his lips. "As long as you don't start a fight, you and the clan are welcome here."

"Oh, we won't start a fight. We'll start a *war* next time," Clement whispered.

Merrick pushed him, and Clement stumbled forward. He snarled, but Merrick merely raised a brow. He looked like he didn't care one bit what Clement and Warner could do to him.

However, Merrick and Arlen cared about what the clan could do. If they decided to take them out, they would. They weren't alone, especially with the vampire conclave entering the fight, but they knew better than anyone how dangerous dragons could be. The clan wouldn't stop at anything to get what they wanted.

Even if it meant killing two former clan members.

CHAPTER TWO

Mallory was just getting up when his phone vibrated. He expected it to be one of his siblings, but the text message came from Oren.

Team meeting in the living room. Ten minutes.

Mallory groaned and flopped back onto his bed. He stared at the ceiling for a moment, trying to give himself the push he needed to get to his feet. He'd stayed at the club way too late last night, until the early hours of the morning. Arlen hadn't been with him the entire time, but Mallory had been stupid enough to stay in the hope that he'd see him again. Now he was exhausted, and he wished he could stay in bed.

Instead, he pushed himself to his feet and headed to the bathroom.

He felt more human once he'd showered, but his stomach growled as he made his way downstairs. He hesitated, wondering if he'd have time to go to the kitchen to grab some blood before the meeting started, but Renata bounced down the stairs behind him, grabbed his arm as she walked past him, and pulled him into the living room.

Apparently, he wouldn't have a choice.

He blinked when he saw that Robin and Baxter were present, too. Robin looked half-asleep like Mallory felt, but Baxter was bouncing on the couch. He grinned when he saw Mallory, exposing his fangs, and he patted the spot next to himself. Mallory gave him a little glare, but he flopped down and leaned against him.

"How are you so awake when we were so late this

morning?" he whined.

"When you live with a wolf, you learn a new sleeping schedule. If I still slept away the entire day, I'd never see Sloan."

"It still doesn't explain how you can be so awake."

Baxter wiggled his eyebrows. "I had the best wake-up call this morning."

Mallory groaned. He supposed he'd earned that. "I don't want to hear about your sex life."

"At least I *have* a sex life. Although with the way you and Arlen were cozying up, maybe you'll have one soon, too."

Mallory didn't even have the energy to glare. Besides, Oren was walking into the living room, looking like his best friend had died. That made Mallory sit up straighter and frown. Whatever was happening, it wasn't good.

Mallory's phone vibrated in his pocket, but he only gave it a quick glance to make sure it wasn't an emergency. His brother Umberto was texting him, but he'd have to wait.

"I spoke to the conclave," Oren said when he had everyone's attention. "They want us to withdraw."

It took a moment for the words to register. Even when they did, Mallory couldn't make sense of them.

"You mean they want you to go back and leave the pack on its own?" Robin asked.

That would explain Oren's grim expression. "Yes."

"But the clan is attacking the pack. Surely, the conclave has to see that the pack needs to be protected."

"They do, but since the pack belongs to wolves, they believe it's not our problem."

"Two of our team members live with the pack," Gladys pointed out.

"I'm only telling you what they told me. Besides, since both Robin and Baxter have left the team and the conclave, they're washing their hands of them. I don't think they're happy that both of them have found happiness with wolves."

"It's still that stupid thing about vampires and wolves hating each other?" Mallory asked.

"That's not how they framed it, but I suspect so. As it is, they decided that whatever happens to the pack isn't their problem. They don't want to antagonize the clan, which I understand, but it means we can't stay and fight with the pack."

"I'm not going anywhere," Renata declared.

Mallory nodded in agreement. What was the conclave thinking? Well, Mallory knew what they were thinking. Some conclave members were nice people who wanted to help everyone, regardless of what kind of supernatural creature they were, but other members wouldn't help a baby satyr if they were dying in front of them. Wolves, especially, were a sore spot for some vampires. Mallory hadn't believed the conclave would do something like this, though. The conclave had been created to protect vampires, and Baxter and Robin were vampires. The conclave needed to protect them if they were in danger, especially from a dragon clan.

But they wouldn't. Oren had been clear about that. The conclave expected them to go back and abandon Baxter and Robin.

Mallory would rather die than do that.

"I quit," he declared loud enough that everyone in the room heard him.

It wasn't easy, because they were talking over each other, except for Baxter, who'd curled into himself. It wasn't like him to be silent, but Mallory understood. Even though Baxter didn't consider the pack his home yet, it was where Sloan lived. If something happened to the pack, something happened to Sloan.

"What are you talking about?" Robin asked.

But Gladys was nodding. "I quit, too," she said. "There's no way I'm going back when Baxter and Robin are in danger.

They're my brothers. I'm not abandoning them, and if the conclave doesn't want to help, that's fine. I just won't work for them anymore."

Oren raised his hands. "It might not come to that."

"Oren, I might have started to work for the conclave because I wanted to save lives, but let's be honest. They only want vampires to be safe, and that's not right," Mallory said. "I'll admit I've been thinking about possibly quitting, especially now that Baxter and Robin have. This is just one more nail in the coffin, and the way they're treating Baxter and Robin, along with the wolves, is telling me they're not people I want to work for."

"I understand," Oren said. "But maybe it doesn't have to come to quitting, at least not in the beginning. I knew none of you would be happy when you found out about this, so I looked into it. We can all ask for a sabbatical."

Mallory knew what it was, but he didn't understand how it would change anything. "I doubt the conclave will be different once we're done with our sabbatical," he pointed out.

"Maybe, maybe not. I'm still hoping that the conclave members who are on our side will be able to make a difference. No matter how much I don't like relying on the conclave, we're going to need help when the clan decides to attack."

"And you think the conclave will help?" Mallory wouldn't have thought so even before, but after what Oren had told them, he *knew* the conclave wouldn't step in. They'd sacrifice vampires so they wouldn't have to help wolves.

"Not every conclave member is an asshole. There are good people there. People who would want to help the entire supernatural community instead of just vampires. We have to give them time to change things from the inside."

"And you think the conclave will accept our requests for sabbaticals?" Gladys asked. "I mean, there's no way they won't know what we're doing."

"I don't care if they know we're staying here to help the pack," Oren told her. "They won't be happy, but they can't refuse our request. And if they do, well, we'll quit, right?"

"I guess."

"We just need to put the requests in. I have everything ready for all of us."

Mallory grinned. "You already knew they were going to do this."

"I suspected it. I have faith in the conclave and what they represent, but not in every conclave member. I do believe things can get better, but it won't happen overnight, and in the meantime, the pack still needs our help."

"So you're staying?" Baxter asked.

Mallory leaned against him. He didn't like it when Baxter was quiet, because it was so different from the man he usually was. When Baxter was silent, it meant something was very wrong, and Mallory hoped that knowing everyone was staying and would help the wolves would make Baxter happy.

Oren nodded. "We're staying, whether you like it or not."

Baxter snorted. "Did you think I was going to say no? This is the best thing that could happen. I just don't want any of you to end up in trouble because of us."

"You let us make that decision. Everyone here knows what they're going up against and what they risk by doing this. The forms are ready, so I'll need all of you to come to me and sign them. I'll send them over to the conclave as soon as you do. You still have time to change your mind."

Mallory looked around the room. Given their expressions, he doubted any of them would decide to go back. They were already involved in this fight, and the only way they'd step away from it was if it was over.

Once again, the club was full. It made the numbers on Arlen's screen a pleasant thing to look at, but they'd lost his attention a few seconds ago. He could hear Merrick stomping in the hallway toward the office, but Arlen didn't think he was alone. He also wasn't muttering about the latest stupid thing one of their customers had done, so Arlen expected that whatever would happen next, he wouldn't like it.

He suspected Merrick knew he was aware of his arrival. Merrick would never have dared walk into the office without knocking otherwise, but today, he threw the door open. He pushed the person he was with forward, and the man stumbled, almost falling on his face. He quickly caught himself and turned to glare at Merrick, but Arlen kept his attention on him.

He was a dragon shifter.

"I caught him selling drugs," Merrick said.

He sounded like he'd gladly tear the dragon apart with his bare hands, which Arlen knew was a reality. If Merrick could get away with killing the drug dealers they found in the club, he would.

Arlen got to his feet, never looking away from the dragon. He was young and trying to behave as if he wasn't afraid. Arlen could see him sweating, though, and his hands trembling. The dragon was terrified, and Arlen didn't blame him.

He walked around his desk and came to stand in front of it. He leaned back, crossed his arms over his chest, and continued staring. More often than not, when he wanted to know what was happening, he didn't have to ask questions. Staring at whoever was involved for long enough would push them to talk.

Tonight wasn't any different.

The dragon raised his chin in a defiant gesture. "You can't touch me," he said. "The clan will kill you if you do."

And there it was. The dragon had just revealed who had

sent him—not that Arlen had expected anything different. The clan wanted him to pay, and now that he'd helped a vampire and had kicked out the bartender who worked as their drug dealer, they'd make it hurt. Arlen wasn't looking forward to it, but he didn't regret what he'd done. He didn't want drugs in his club, and even more importantly, he didn't want the clan to stick their nose in his business. He'd left the clan for a reason, and while he'd always known that eventually they would retaliate, he hadn't expected it to happen in these circumstances.

"Shut your mouth," Merrick growled.

The dragon folded in on himself just a bit. "You can't hurt me," he said again as if repeating himself would help.

"Is that what they told you?" Arlen asked. "That if we caught you, we'd hurt you?"

"Fuck you," the dragon spat out.

Merrick reached out and hit him over the back of the head. He put enough force into it to make the dragon stumble, but it didn't hurt, if the dragon's glare toward Merrick was an indication of anything.

Arlen pinched the bridge of his nose. "The clan should know better. The club is mine, and I won't allow anyone to deal drugs here, not even them."

The dragon snorted. "What you want and what you allow doesn't matter. The clan does what they want when they want to do it. You don't stand a chance against them."

Arlen suspected he was right. If Arlen and Merrick had to face the clan on their own, it wouldn't end well for them. It would have been easier to close the club and leave, but Arlen wasn't about to do that. Even if he was killed resisting the clan, he wasn't giving them the satisfaction of making him run away.

That meant he was going to have to talk to the clan leader. He wasn't looking forward to it. The man had been an asshole even when Arlen was a clan member, and he doubted things had changed. Besides, considering how he was leading the clan, there was a good chance that whatever Arlen tried to say wouldn't be welcome. The clan leader had never allowed anyone to intervene in his decisions, and while he hadn't been able to stop Arlen and Merrick from leaving, he could decide to make their lives a living hell for doing so. He hadn't until now because the clan had still been hiding, but that looked like that was over, and eventually, the clan would make sure the entire supernatural community in the area knew about them.

That was when the problems would start.

Arlen waved at Merrick. "Take him outside and confiscate the drugs. Destroy them." He turned his attention back to the dragon. "I won't be as nice the next time I catch you here dealing drugs. You've been warned."

"The clan won't let you do this."

"Yeah?" Merrick asked. He slapped the dragon again. "Then please, tell them I slapped you upside the head a few times. I can't wait to see what they're going to do about it."

Merrick grabbed the dragon and dragged him out of the office. Arlen could hear the dragon protest, and while he doubted the clan would step in for such a young dragon, especially considering the situation they'd put him in, he couldn't say he wasn't worried. The clan was testing his boundaries, and he needed to be firm if he wanted to stand a chance against them.

Arlen was still thinking when Merrick came back. He was carrying enough drugs to kill half the vampires in the club. He made a beeline for the bathroom, and Arlen heard him throw everything into the toilet and flush a few times.

These drugs wouldn't hurt anyone, but what about the others? He had no doubt the clan was still producing them and that he'd see them in his club again, and soon.

"Whatever you're thinking, don't do it," Merrick said as he left the bathroom.

Arlen arched a brow. "What do you think I'm thinking?"

"I don't know, but it's not good. I can tell from your expression."

Arlen sighed. "I have to contact the clan."

Merrick shook his head. "Nope. You don't have to do anything. You especially don't have to contact the clan, because that would be a stupid thing to do."

"It's the only thing I can do. They targeted us. They'll expect a reaction, and I have to give it to them."

"We're not clan members anymore, and there's a good reason for that. You know what will happen if you go against them so openly."

"I do. But do we have a choice? We can't ignore what just happened. It would only give the clan the impression that we can't do anything against them and that they can do whatever they want."

"Because contacting them will change that? They'll do what they want, anyway. They don't care about us, Arlen. Actually, that's bullshit. They do care about us in the sense that they want us dead. They won't stop for anything to make that happen, and I don't want to lose you."

"I don't want to lose you or the club, which is why I need to do this."

Merrick squared his shoulders. "Then I'm coming with you."

Arlen didn't try to dissuade him. He knew his best friend wouldn't let him do something so dangerous on his own, and even though it put Merrick in danger, he was glad for that. He wasn't sure he'd have the guts to face the clan on his own.

"Let's go, then," he murmured.

"You think they'll see us at this hour of the night?"

Arlen and Merrick kept a nocturnal schedule for necessity,

since they owned the club, but the clan didn't. "Do you care if we wake them up?"

"No, but they'll already be pissed enough. Is it wise to make it worse by waking them up?"

"Probably not, but I can't let this go. Besides, their little drug dealer is probably running home as we speak. They'll know what happened, and they'll know to expect us." And Arlen wanted to get it out of the way.

As he and Merrick headed out after putting one of the bouncers in charge, Arlen slid his phone out of his pocket. He didn't think the clan would kill him and Merrick tonight, but just in case, he texted Mallory to tell him what had happened and what Arlen was about to do. He hoped he'd have the opportunity to see Mallory again and explore whatever had sparked between them the night before, but that would depend on what happened next. At least this way, Mallory would know he wasn't ghosting him.

Because possibly by the time this was over, he'd *be* a ghost.

Even though Mallory was going along with Oren's plan, he wondered if it would be better to quit the conclave entirely. Oren had faith that eventually the conclave would fix itself, but Mallory wasn't so sure. He supposed that Oren needed to believe that since he'd been a conclave enforcer for so long, but Mallory didn't feel the same loyalty as Oren. He understood the need for the conclave and agreed with their mission to keep vampires safe, but the world had changed. The conclave needed to accept that and open up to the idea that vampires needed other supernatural communities.

But he didn't have to make that decision now. He and the others were on sabbatical, which meant they could focus on protecting the pack and dealing with the clan. Mallory wasn't sure how they'd do it, but now, they had time to come up with a plan.

His phone kept vibrating in his pocket, but he was sure it was one of his siblings, if not more than one of them. With eight of them, there was always someone texting to chat or sending funny pictures they found on the Internet. Cressida especially tended to do that, and always when Mallory couldn't look at the pictures. Then she'd get pissed. She just couldn't understand that Mallory had a job to do and couldn't spend half of his day answering her texts.

But after the meeting with Oren, the team now had a meeting with Kieran. Robin had gone to fetch his boyfriend, and Kieran sat on the edge of one of the armchairs in their living room, looking around as if he expected one of them to attack him. He was wary, which was understandable, but Mallory wished Kieran didn't look like he didn't trust them.

"Robin told me the conclave ordered you to return," Kieran said.

At least that explained why he looked like he'd gotten bad news.

Oren nodded. "They did, but I just sent off the forms for all of us to take a sabbatical. We're still conclave enforcers, but we won't be working for the conclave in the short term."

Kieran nodded. "Robin mentioned something about that, too. I'm glad that you're not going anywhere, because I need all the help I can get, but I admit I don't understand. You're conclave enforcers. You should follow the conclave's orders."

"We would if their orders made sense," Mallory told him. "But as it is, they're asking us to abandon our brothers. None of us are ready to do that."

"If our presence with the pack is a problem, we can find another place to stay in town," Oren intervened.

He glanced at Mallory. Mallory had worked with him for long enough that he knew it was Oren's *shut-up* glance. He raised his hands to tell Oren he'd understood and that he'd keep his mouth shut, at least for now.

"I doubt that having you stay with us longer will make much of a difference. Some pack members will still be pissed by your presence, but those who don't care won't change their mind about it. No, you can stay and use this house for as long as you need to."

"Thank you."

Kieran shook his head and got to his feet. "It should be me thanking you. I understand you're mainly doing this for Robin and Baxter, but I'm still grateful. I've never dealt with dragons, and honestly, I'm not quite sure what will happen."

"I don't think anyone is," Baxter pointed out. "But at least we won't be facing these people alone, right? Right now, it's all that matters."

"I suppose it is. I still need to email the entire pack, just in case. I'm the alpha, and I make the decisions, but I know enough to be aware of the fact that some of the members might give us trouble. They don't understand how important it is for us to keep you here. They only see their comfort and beliefs, without looking at the bigger picture."

The bigger picture being the dragons attacking the wolves. No matter how numerous the pack was, they wouldn't be able to fend off an entire clan of dragons.

Kieran took his phone out of his pocket. He looked like someone had just told him his dog had died, and while Mallory hadn't interacted much with the pack members, he understood why Kieran felt that way. Most pack members were perfectly nice, if a bit wary and puzzled about their presence here, but some were unhappy to have their team with the pack. Mallory just had to think about the wolf he'd encountered in the forest the other night. They'd snarled at him, ensuring he understood he wasn't welcome.

Unfortunately for the wolves, Mallory and the other vampires were here to stay. They'd just have to get used to it.

Kieran barely had time to send his email before his phone started ringing. Mallory was grateful he wasn't in Kieran's place, but Robin kind of was. Even though he was a vampire, he was the alpha mate, and Mallory had no doubt that some pack members would point at him as part of the problem. He wished he could do more to help his friend, but things were what they were, and as long as they didn't have to fight the pack as well as the clan, things would be okay.

Or at least, Mallory hoped that would be the case.

His hope died a few seconds later. Something slammed against the front door, sending all of them to their feet. Mallory's heart raced at the thought that the clan might be attacking, but when Oren threw open the door, it was to find a woman standing just off the porch. Her blonde hair had escaped the messy bun on top of her head and framed her face — her angry face. Her cheeks were flushed, and her eyes looked like they might kill someone. Her hands were balled into fists by her side, and she looked ready to fight.

But she stayed where she was. She waited until Kieran exited the house, and her full attention went to him. "What are you thinking?" she demanded to know.

Mallory noticed a rock on the porch just by the door. Had she thrown it to get them to come outside?

"That I'm the alpha, and I'm the one making decisions," he said.

"I'm your *sister*. Shouldn't you consult me? Shouldn't you consult our father, who was the alpha until you decided you had enough?"

Mallory cringed. This would be even worse than he'd expected. He hadn't known Kieran had trouble with his family. After all, his brother was his beta, and the two of them worked together pretty well.

Mallory expected Kieran to be disappointed, but his expression had gone stony. He stood on the porch, staring at his sister as if he hadn't heard her words.

"As the alpha, I don't need to consult anyone when I make decisions, not you, our father, or even my beta. *I* make the decisions alone, and if you can't respect that, you know where the door is."

"You'll ruin the pack," his sister spat out. "You're making us work with these vampires. You gave the bloodsuckers a home, and now, you're telling us they'll be living with us? It was bad enough that both you and Sloan chose to be with vampires. Why does the pack have to deal with these bloodsuckers, too?"

"You don't know the entire story, Fay. I realize you're angry, even though I don't share the feelings behind it. But I'm your alpha, and you need to trust me. We have enemies out there, *dragons*, and they won't stop until they destroy us. We need all the help we can find, and this team of vampires has offered to stand up for us."

"We don't need them! I don't care who wants to destroy us, because the pack is too strong for them to hurt us."

"You don't know anything about the situation. Stop fooling yourself that you know what's happening."

She pointed a finger at Kieran. "I won't stand for this. I didn't say anything when you pushed our father out, but this is too much. And I'm not alone, so be ready to face our anger. The pack is ours, and we won't allow you to sully it with these vampires."

Kieran looked like he wanted to answer her, but he didn't get the chance. She turned around and stomped away, but Mallory suspected they'd hear from her again, and he wasn't looking forward to it. What she'd said could mean trouble for him and his team, and they already had enough of that with the dragons.

Arlen looked up at the house. He'd thought he'd never come back, and he wished he hadn't. He'd grown up here, but most of his memories of the place were unhappy.

"You're so sure you want to do this?" Merrick asked.

"No, but I don't have a choice. I need to show the clan that I'm not afraid of them."

Merrick snorted. "I'm not. They're dickheads."

His words made Arlen smile, which Arlen sorely needed. "You're not wrong. Still, there's a chance they won't take our presence here nicely. You should stay out here."

Merrick shook his head and opened the passenger door of Arlen's car. "I'm not letting you face them alone."

That was what Arlen had hoped to hear, but it didn't mean he didn't worry about his friend. He'd never forgive himself if something happened to Merrick because of him, but they didn't have a choice anymore. They were here, and he needed to talk to the clan leader.

With a sigh, Arlen followed Merrick out of the car.

"How are we doing this?" Merrick asked as they both stared at the house again. "I can be the bad cop."

"I'm sure. But I think you should let me speak."

"Yeah, I wasn't going to try to convince these assholes to leave us alone. I didn't have any patience for them when I left, and that hasn't changed. If they try to hurt you, though, all bets are off. I'll be kicking ass, even if it kills me."

It just might. Still, there was no going back, so Arlen strode toward the front door instead of rushing back to the car as he desperately wanted. He hoped he looked unafraid. He'd worked a lot to hide his facial expressions, but this was the first time he truly needed to look like he knew what he was talking about.

The front door opened before they reached it. A woman stood there, glaring at them as if they'd killed her cat. Arlen would have recognized her anywhere.

Virginia, the second in command.

Her black hair was cut into a bob that framed her face in a too-severe cut. She didn't wear makeup or jewelry, but then, Arlen remembered she believed they were futile. Like always, she wore all black, possibly because you couldn't see blood-stains on that color.

"The two of you left the clan. You have no place here." Her voice was unforgiving, her tone harsh.

Arlen didn't think she ever talked differently. He'd always heard her speak like this, and he couldn't help but wonder if, as a child, she'd done so, too. He almost laughed at the image it created in his mind, but the last thing he needed was for Virginia to think he was making fun of her.

"We're here to talk to Gerald," he said.

"Why should he talk to you? You're not a clan member anymore."

"Does that mean Gerald only talks to clan members? I seem to remember he has business associates all over town."

"But you're not one of them. What do you want?"

"We found one of your men dealing drugs in my club earlier. I'm sure he's already run to you to tell you what happened."

"He told me you destroyed our drugs."

"And I'll continue to destroy them if I find more of them in my club."

"You're welcome to do what you want. You owe us, though. Those drugs are expensive."

"Then you shouldn't deal them in my club." The clan didn't just deal in deadly drugs, but Arlen couldn't risk it, especially when they'd already targeted vampires recently.

"Are you going to leave us standing here the entire time?" Merrick asked. He sounded bored, but Arlen knew he was anything but.

"Gerald is on his way. You can wait outside until he gets

here. He'll decide what to do with you."

At least it would be easier for them to escape if they were out here. Arlen hadn't been looking forward to going into the house, and he was glad he wouldn't have to.

So the three of them stayed there, glaring at each other. Virginia didn't say anything else, but Arlen could almost see the hatred pouring off her. He didn't understand what he'd done to make her hate him so much. He didn't care, either. He just wanted the clan to stay out of his life and his club, and while he doubted that would happen, at least he was trying.

"Well, well, well, look who came crawling back," a male voice said.

Arlen gritted his teeth. He needed to remember that punching Gerald in his smug face would only create more trouble for him and Merrick. Still, the urge was there when Gerald appeared next to Virginia.

Where she was dark, he was light. His blond hair was neatly cut and styled, and, with his white jeans and shirt, he was so bright that it almost hurt Arlen's eyes. He looked like a top model who'd just stepped off the catwalk, and while he was beautiful on the outside, inside, he was rotten. His blue eyes sparkled with anger and animosity, and the way he looked at Arlen made Arlen's skin crawl.

"I didn't think I'd ever see you again," Gerald said. "If I remember correctly, your last words were that you'd be better off on your own than with the clan."

Arlen straightened his shoulders. "And I still believe that. We're here because you're selling drugs in my club."

Gerald slowly climbed down the steps. Virginia followed him as if she were afraid Arlen was going to try to hurt him, and she wouldn't be wrong. Arlen still wanted to punch Gerald's perfect face until his outside looked like his inside.

"Are we?" Gerald asked.

"You know damn well you are. We found your dragon. We

destroyed the drugs, by the way."

Anger flashed in Gerald's expression, but it was gone almost as quickly as it appeared. "Well, that's a pity. They would have earned us quite a bit of money. Of course, we don't exactly need it. As I'm sure you remember, the clan is wealthy."

"I'd appreciate it if you stopped selling drugs in my club," Arlen said. "I know that some of those drugs are deadly for vampires and other supernatural creatures, and I don't want my customers dying in the club."

"I suppose that would make for a messy cleanup. Are you asking me for a favor, then?"

Arlen had to be careful. If he agreed that he was asking Gerald a favor, Gerald would take advantage of that. He'd never let it go, and Arlen would be indebted to him for the rest of his life. Gerald knew what he was doing, but so did Arlen.

"Not a favor. This is just a warning that if we find more of your drugs in the club, we'll destroy those, too. As wealthy as the clan is, I don't know how much drugs you can afford to lose before you start getting in trouble."

"Are you threatening me?"

Arlen forced himself to smile. "It's not a threat. It's a warning of what will happen if you continue what you've been doing. You're free to do so, but you'll have to deal with the consequences if you do."

Arlen didn't wait for an answer. He turned around, and while he could feel Merrick behind him, he didn't turn to make sure his friend was okay. He also didn't check whether or not Virginia or Gerald were going to attack. He trusted Merrick to have his back.

He slipped back into the driver seat of his car, waited for Merrick to join him in the passenger seat, and turned the engine on. He needed to get out of here as soon as possible. Just being so close to the clan made his stomach churn, and he swore he could feel Gerald's gaze on the back of his neck until he turned the corner.

"I suppose it could have gone worse," Merrick said.

Arlen barked out a laugh. "As in, they could have killed us?"

"Well, yes. But we're still here."

They were, but Arlen couldn't help but wonder for how long they would be. If the clan decided to destroy them, they would, and nothing Arlen and Merrick could do would change the outcome.

CHAPTER THREE

It was odd not to have specific orders about what to do. Mallory supposed Oren could give the team orders, but he technically wasn't their leader right now. None of them would care, but they were at the point in their mission where they had to wait and see what happened next. They couldn't take the first step and attack the dragons, which meant they had to see what the dragons would do.

It had always been Mallory's most hated part of the missions.

"Do you think we should have someone at the club every night?" Baxter suddenly asked. He was sitting on the couch next to Mallory.

Mallory blinked at him. Most of the team was gathered in the living room they shared, and while Baxter technically wasn't a team member anymore, he spent a lot of time with them. Sloan slept part of the night, and Baxter didn't want to be alone.

"Why do you think we need to have someone there?" Oren asked.

"Well, Arlen says they're fine, but he also mentioned that when he and Merrick left the clan, the clan wasn't happy. They're focusing on the pack, but I wouldn't be surprised if they tried something with the club. There was that fight the other night, and the guy who started it is a clan dragon."

Oren looked thoughtful. Mallory could tell that he felt uneasy with their inaction, too, so he wasn't surprised when eventually, Oren nodded.

"It's not a bad idea. If the clan is going to attack the club, we should have someone there. If anything, it would be good to have someone to help get the customers out of the club." He looked around the living room. "But if the club is attacked, that's all you need to focus on. We can't afford to face the dragons yet, not when we don't know their plan."

"Pretty sure their plan is to kill everyone in the pack," Gladys muttered.

"I agree, but we'll be the aggressors if we attack them. We'll be in the wrong, and we can't afford that."

Baxter clicked his tongue. "Not that I disagree with you, but I don't think anyone would care if we were in the wrong. I mean, every supernatural creature in town knows about the clan now that they started poking around and exposing themselves, and I'm pretty sure they know the clan is behind the death of the vampires who took those drugs. No one likes the dragons."

"We can't risk it. We need allies, and I'm still working on that. The team alone won't be enough to attack the clan, and I don't want any of you to get hurt because you did something stupid."

"We won't do anything stupid," Baxter promised. "We'll go to the club, sit in a corner, and drink a little blood. We'll keep an eye on the crowd, and if Arlen and Merrick need us, we'll step in. I just dislike leaving them on their own, especially after what Arlen did for me."

"You think the clan is angry at him for that?"

Baxter shrugged. "I don't know what the clan thinks, and honestly, I don't care. It just doesn't sit well with me that we're leaving them in danger."

Oren sighed. "Why don't you and Mallory go there tonight? There are still several hours before morning."

To no one's surprise, Baxter shot to his feet. "We'll head there right now."

Mallory was slower following him. He wanted to see Arlen and make sure he was okay, but he didn't want to be obvious about it.

After the meeting where Oren had told them the conclave wasn't allowing them to stay in an official capacity and handed out the forms to take a sabbatical, Mallory had finally looked at who had been texting him. Most of the texts had been from his family members, but there had been one from Arlen. They'd exchanged numbers the night they'd met, and Mallory had been glad to see Arlen's name on a screen. Then he'd read the text and realized that Arlen had been in danger.

And he hadn't even known.

He felt guilty. Arlen had sent him a message to let him know he was going to face the clan because they'd found another drug dealer at the club. He'd known it would be dangerous, and he'd wanted Mallory to know where he and Merrick were, just in case something happened. Instead of being there for him, Mallory had ignored it. As soon as he'd seen Arlen's message, he'd texted back, ready to step in, but Arlen had reassured him that the meeting had been a disaster, but no one had been hurt. Mallory had yet to see him again, and he was glad he would tonight.

"So, how are things going between you and Arlen?" Baxter asked once they were out of the house.

"There's nothing between us."

"Try to tell someone else that. Come on. I was there the night you met, and I could see the sparks flying between the two of you. Have you seen him again yet?"

"When would I have?"

Mallory and Baxter climbed into Sloan's truck. Since the team was staying, they'd have to get their own vehicles, and Mallory was looking forward to it. He didn't like depending on anyone, even people he trusted.

"You tell me. You've been here a few nights now."

41

"Yes, and we spent all our time talking things out between us, then contacting the conclave."

Even though they'd only had to send in the requests for their sabbatical, things had gotten complicated. Several conclave members had called Oren to find out what was happening, and while a few had been okay with the team staying back to help Robin and Baxter and the wolves, some had been pissed. Mallory could swear his ears still rang from the screaming coming from Oren's phone. He'd been glad not to be the team leader at that moment.

They'd needed to do some damage control, and they had. Then, last night, they'd all stayed in pack territory. There was a bit of unrest with the wolves, and Oren had thought it prudent not to show themselves too much. Mallory thought that even if they didn't, the wolves could still see Robin and Baxter, but he hadn't said anything. They were dating the alpha and the beta, and the pack needed to learn to deal with that.

Mallory couldn't even begin to imagine what it was like. He didn't want to have authority over anyone, let alone a pack of wolves. Robin was braver than he ever could be, and while he was in awe of his friend, he also understood how hard this was for both Robin and Baxter. They weren't just leaving their old lives and everyone they cared about behind. If it was only that, Mallory wouldn't have been worried. That was what vampires did routinely, anyway.

But the two of them had to live with the pack, and not every pack member was accepting. They also had to behave like the alpha mate and the beta's mate, and with a group of people who didn't trust them, it couldn't be easy. They couldn't avoid those responsibilities, though. Mallory suspected the wolves would have been even more pissed if they'd tried.

"Have you talked to him on the phone, then?" Baxter asked. "Or at least texted him?"

"We *have* been texting. The night we had that meeting with Oren and sent in our sabbaticals, Arlen texted me to tell me he was going to the clan."

Baxter sucked in a breath and briefly looked away from the road. Thankfully, he turned his attention back to it almost immediately. "Why did he do that?"

"He and Merrick found a dragon dealing drugs in the club. He thought it would be best to face the clan and show them he wasn't afraid of them."

"No one thought he was afraid of them."

"I certainly didn't, but we have no way to know what dragons think."

"He and Merrick are both okay, though, right?"

"Yes. We texted last night, too, and they're fine."

"That's good." Baxter hesitated. "You know, I wish the entire team would stay. I don't want to lose any of you just because I found Sloan."

"Even if we have to go back, you won't lose us. You're too important to all of us."

"I know. But it won't be the same."

There was nothing Mallory could say about that. He didn't know what would happen once all of this was over, but Baxter was right when he said it wouldn't be the same. They'd lost two team members, and Mallory was seriously considering leaving the team. He didn't like the way the conclave was behaving, and he didn't have much keeping him in the city except for the team. His family lived in different cities, so that wouldn't keep him there.

If he stayed, he'd have Baxter and Robin.

And maybe, Arlen.

Arlen had been watching the feed from inside the club from his office. He told himself it was because he wanted to make sure no dragon tried to sneak in, but in reality, he hoped Mallory would come around.

Mallory hadn't said anything about coming to the club. They'd been texting on and off for the past few nights, and while it had given Arlen the urge to get to know Mallory better, so far, the texts had been the only way they'd communicated. He wanted to know more, but he didn't want to be invasive, and after all, Mallory was here for work, not for pleasure.

But Arlen still perked up when he saw Mallory and Baxter enter the club on the screen. He followed their path through the club until they sat at a small table by the bar. They didn't seem to be here to dance and have fun, which meant they were here for work. That was kind of a pity, but at least Arlen would see Mallory.

He got to his feet, spent a few minutes in his bathroom making sure he looked okay, then pushed his office door open. There was no one in the hallway, but then, no one was supposed to be there. It led to his office, the break room, and the room where they kept their supplies, so no customer should be around.

The sound of music became louder the closer he got to the dance floor. He knew where he was going, so he didn't waste any time crossing the dance floor. He paused at the bar to give the order that whatever Mallory and Baxter ordered was on the house. Then he strode toward their table.

Baxter and Mallory hadn't seen him yet, which gave him the opportunity to watch them. It was clear the two of them were close, but from the way they behaved, it was like brothers and nothing more. Besides, Baxter was dating Sloan. But the way they were with each other spoke of deep love and trust, something Arlen could understand. He felt the same way about Merrick.

Mallory looked up, and their gazes met. Arlen found

himself smiling, and he couldn't stop, even when he reached the table.

"Good evening," he told both of them.

Baxter beamed at him. "Hey."

Mallory's smile was more reserved, but it was there, and there was something in it that told Arlen that Mallory was happy to see him.

"I told the bar that anything you order is on the house," he said.

He wasn't sure how to behave. He didn't date, and he hadn't thought he was ready to do so. He wasn't even sure if what he wanted from Mallory was dating. That sounded too normal, too tame. He wanted to be with Mallory, but did they really have to date to get to know each other, or could they go straight to the part where they ended up in bed and fell in love?

"You didn't have to do that," Mallory said.

"It doesn't mean I didn't want to do it. Can I ask what you two gentlemen are doing here tonight?"

"We thought it would be a good idea to have someone from the team hanging around every evening," Baxter explained. "You've been having troubles with the dragons, and while we don't think we can face them yet, the least we can do is be here to help if something happens."

It touched Arlen to know that the vampires wanted to protect them, even though he didn't fully understand why. It couldn't be because of his budding relationship with Mallory, but what other reason could there be?

Baxter wagged his finger at Arlen. "I can see what you're thinking."

Arlen arched a brow. "Can you?"

"Yes. It's the same expression Sloan and Kieran had when Oren told them that the team would be staying, even though the conclave disagreed with that decision."

"What expression is that?"

"You don't understand why we're doing it. You're relieved because you know you need help, but you're also confused."

Arlen hadn't thought he was so easily readable. "You're not wrong. I don't understand why you and your team are so interested in helping me."

"Well, we're enforcers. We help anyone who needs help," Mallory said.

"But we're not vampires."

Mallory shrugged. "Who cares? I became an enforcer because I needed something to do with my life and wanted to help people. We're here to help the pack, but that doesn't mean we can't help someone else while we do so, especially when our enemy is the same."

Baxter nodded enthusiastically. "Besides, I like you."

"I like you, too," Arlen told him. He didn't usually like people so easily, but something about Baxter pulled Arlen in. He had a sunny personality and seemed to want to make friends with everyone. It could be a dangerous way to live, but he didn't seem to care — or maybe he did, but not enough to push people away.

Baxter's smile widened. "And you like Mallory, too, right?"

Arlen's gaze moved to Mallory. The vampire wasn't looking at him, but a smile played on his lips.

"And I like Mallory," Arlen confessed.

Baxter was smiling so widely that Arlen couldn't help but wonder if he would end up stuck that way. "Good! Why don't the two of you head to the dance floor then?"

That wasn't what Arlen had expected. "I'm sorry?"

"You heard me. We're here to keep an eye on everything, and while it's great to do so from this table, maybe it would help to have someone on the dance floor. You and Mallory can go there, dance for a bit, and keep an eye on people."

It wasn't something Arlen usually did. He mostly stayed in his office during the evenings. He didn't mind doing the books and buying supplies. He wasn't one to mingle with people, and while Merrick wasn't, either, he didn't mind the noise and the crowd. As long as people stayed away from him — which they did because he looked uncompromising — he was fine, and he could keep an eye on the customers and the club.

But Arlen found himself offering Mallory his hand. "Shall we?"

Mallory looked from Baxter to Arlen's hand. He thought about it for a moment, then he nodded. Arlen's heart tripped when he reached out and their fingers touched.

"Stay at the table," Mallory ordered.

"I'm not going anywhere," Baxter promised. "You make sure to keep an eye out for enemies or whatever."

Mallory rolled his eyes and pulled Arlen toward the dance floor. They stayed at its fringe, but that was fine with Arlen. It was especially fine when Mallory hooked an arm around his waist and pulled him close, even when he realized it was so that Mallory could whisper in his ear.

"You know he didn't do this because he thought it would be good for us to keep an eye on the club, right?"

Arlen chuckled. "I do. He was kind of obvious."

"He means well. He's happy with Sloan, and he wants everyone to be as happy as he is."

Mallory had to lean close enough that his lips brushed Arlen's ear every time he spoke. Otherwise, Arlen wouldn't have been able to hear what he was saying. The closeness of Mallory's body and the warm breath on his skin made Arlen shudder, and, instead of stepping away, Mallory moved even closer. They pressed together, shuffling their feet in a circle instead of dancing, and while they had to look like idiots, Arlen didn't care.

He was in Mallory's arms, and that was all he'd wanted since he'd first met the vampire.

Mallory's mouth was still by Arlen's ear, but Arlen slowly turned his face. His cheek scraped against Mallory's in the most delicious way. Mallory did the same until they were staring at each other. Mallory's gaze flickered to Arlen's lips, and Arlen found himself licking them even though he hadn't meant to. The hunger that flared in Mallory's eyes told him that whatever he was about to do would be welcome.

So he kissed Mallory.

He wanted to do so much more, but they were in public, so he limited himself to pressing their lips together. The problems started when Mallory opened his mouth to him, welcoming him inside. Arlen's tongue scraped against one of Mallory's fangs, and Arlen shuddered again. What would it feel like to have Mallory bite him while they were having sex? It wasn't something Arlen had ever thought about, but he couldn't stop now. Did he really want a vampire to bite him?

Yes, if that vampire was Mallory.

If Mallory had known that kissing Arlen would feel so good, he'd have done it the night they met. At least he'd only wasted two days not worshipping Arlen. Arlen didn't even seem to care about Mallory's fangs. Mallory knew he'd felt them, and there was no way for him to hide them. Arlen didn't make him feel like he had to, though. He made Mallory feel like he could be himself, which didn't often happen when Mallory was with someone who wasn't a vampire.

He raised his free hand and cupped it around the back of Arlen's head. He deepened the kiss, almost forgetting where they were standing. They'd stopped attempting to dance, and they felt like an island in the middle of a flood.

Someone landed against his back. At the same time, a

scream rose, high enough that it could be heard above the music.

Mallory wrenched away from Arlen and looked around. His eyes widened when he realized why the person had been screaming.

"What the fuck are they thinking?" Arlen yelled. He was already pushing his way through the panicking crowd toward the shifting dragon.

Mallory wanted to go with him, but he and Baxter were here for a reason, so instead, he started pushing people toward the entrance. He made sure the doors were open, and he found that Merrick was guiding the people who'd been dancing just a few seconds ago through the exit. Their gazes caught, and Merrick nodded before turning back to what he was doing.

The music abruptly cut off. It left Mallory's ears ringing, but at least now, it was easier to hear what was happening around him. The screams of the people trying to save themselves weren't helping, but Mallory focused on getting as many people toward the entrance as possible. At the same time, he moved toward the dragon, who was now in their full dragon form.

Mallory had never seen a dragon shifter in their dragon form, which was impressive. The problem was that the dragon wasn't small, and while there were fewer people in the club, it was still a tight fit. The dragon had sent people to the floor, knocked into tables and chairs, and spilled drinks everywhere. Their skin glistened under the strobing lights, and when they raised their head and roared, the entire building felt like it was shaking.

The dragon's snout was long, with spikes running from the tip of their mouth, up past their nostrils, then their eyes. The spikes widened until they almost looked like horns when they reached the dragon's forehead. There was skin connecting them there, red like the rest of the dragon's flesh. The spikes also ran under the dragon's snout, although there, they were shorter. The dragon's skin was scaly, a mix of red and black, just like their eyes. They had four paws and two wings, and the spikes ran from their head all the way down to the tip of their tail. The red and black of their skin made them look even more intimidating, almost like a demon risen from the depths of hell.

Someone pushed Mallory aside as they ran toward the dragon. Mallory almost attempted to keep them back, but he realized it was Merrick, and since Merrick and Arlen were dragon shifters, they'd be better at dealing with the dragon than Mallory ever could be. Mallory might be a vampire, but the dragon could easily stomp all over him and kill him if they tried.

"Do you see anyone else?" Baxter asked as he rushed toward Mallory.

Mallory looked around. There was no way for them to know if there was anyone in the bathrooms, but he hoped that if there was, they'd be smart enough to stay where they were. The bartenders were still behind the bar, one of them holding a baseball bat, but they didn't move. Mallory hoped they'd gotten everyone out, which meant it was time for them to follow. He turned toward the dragon only to see that Merrick was shifting, too.

The dragon had taken a step toward Arlen, and Merrick hadn't taken it well. He shifted faster than the other dragon had. Smoke billowed from his nose as he opened his mouth wide, exposing his fangs. The sight made Mallory shudder in horror. He wasn't afraid of Merrick, but it was too easy to imagine what those fangs could do to him or anyone else Merrick decided to kill.

That seemed to give pause to the other dragon, too. This dragon was slightly smaller, and while that didn't mean

Merrick would win in a fight, it was clear the dragon didn't want to tempt fate. The fact that they were both stuck in the club also didn't help.

Merrick took a step toward the dragon, who quickly moved back. Their wing hit one of the tables, sending it flying. The dragon snarled and spat fire in Merrick's direction, but Merrick managed to move out of the way before it could hit him. Mallory wasn't sure if the fire would have burned him, but it certainly burned the tables and chairs behind him.

It felt like it only took a second. The fire landed, and it was high, already licking the walls. Mallory frantically looked around, found the closest fire extinguisher, and grabbed it. He couldn't get to the fire because the dragons were in the middle of the dance floor. There was barely enough space for them to move, yet somehow, they seemed to manage it quite easily. Merrick swiped a paw at the dragon's face, and when the dragon moved away, they hit Arlen.

Mallory cried out, pushed the fire extinguisher into Baxter's hands, and rushed to Arlen's side.

He realized it was a bad idea almost right away when he had to dance out of the way of Merrick's wing when he swung it toward the other dragon. Mallory dove under the wing, rolled, and got back to his feet, praying he'd avoided the worst. He could feel pieces of glass embedded in his back, but he didn't pause to check if he was bleeding. He was pretty sure he was, but it didn't matter.

The dragons were still fighting, swiping wings and paws at each other's faces. Mallory dove forward again when a paw brushed against the top of his head. He landed on his knees and slid forward, and since he was almost by Arlen's side, he continued on all fours. Pieces of wood and glass embedded themselves into his skin, but he didn't care.

Arlen was just sitting up when Mallory reached him. Blood dripped from the corner of his mouth, but from what Mallory could see, it was the only sign he'd been hit.

Mallory grabbed Arlen's face. "Are you okay?"

Arlen nodded and struggled to get to his feet. "Is everyone out?"

"Yes, but the club is on fire. We need to leave."

Arden's eyes widened, and he looked around. Baxter had found a second fire extinguisher and was using that one now. The first was discarded by his feet, but unfortunately, neither of them seemed to have done much good. The fire had spread, jumping from chairs to tables to dripping alcohol. It was close enough to the bar that Mallory was getting worried, but at least the bartenders had realized what was happening and had left.

"Grab Baxter and get out of here," Arlen ordered.

"I can't leave you here. You're hurt."

Arlen wiped the blood from his face. "I'm fine, but I can't risk you and Baxter getting hurt."

"What about you and Merrick?"

Arlen turned toward the fighting dragons. There was a long scratch running down Merrick's face now, while the other dragon had folded one of their wings and was holding it close to their body as if it hurt to extend it.

The dragon turned around, swiping their tail at Merrick's head. Merrick dipped, but there wasn't enough space for him to move entirely out of the way. He grunted when the tail hit him on the side of the head. Arlen rushed forward without answering Mallory. He shifted as he did so, and Mallory's eyes widened when he realized what was about to happen.

There was no way this place could hold three fully shifted dragons without exploding.

He ran to Baxter, who'd stopped trying to put the fire out and looked a bit lost. Mallory grabbed his arm and pulled him toward the exit as the room behind him filled with the sound of things cracking and exploding.

There was nothing Baxter and Mallory could do for Merrick and Arlen, no matter how much they wanted to help. They'd done what they were supposed to do, and now, the one thing they needed to focus on was to save themselves.

It was useless to the fight, but the first thing Arlen did once he was in his dragon form was raise his head high and roar. He was angry because he'd lost his club and terrified that Merrick would get hurt. He wanted the dragon who'd attacked them to know that and to fear him.

There wasn't enough space for the three of them to be here, but the fire wouldn't hurt them. Since the club was already ruined, Arlen didn't care about the damage they could do. He also didn't care if the club burned down as long as Merrick made it out in one piece. He was already bleeding, and Arlen wouldn't allow this to continue.

Merrick had always taken the role of protector between them, but that didn't mean Arlen couldn't fight. He couldn't use his wings, but he could use his paws, and he used the strength of his back legs to push himself forward. The other dragon didn't know whether to watch Merrick or Arlen, and a split second of his focus on Merrick was all Arlen needed. He raised his paw high, his claws glinting in the firelight, and swiped it down the dragon's face. He didn't stop there. He reared back, then hit the dragon in the chest.

The dragon screeched in pain, but Arlen didn't step away. He jumped just in time to avoid the dragon's tail, but the dragon slapped him with their wing when he landed.

The fire licked the walls, rising high in the room. It wouldn't be long before the entire building was engulfed, and while Arlen and Merrick couldn't get hurt by the fire, it could spread to other buildings around them. Arlen didn't want the humans in this town or anyone else to pay for what was happening. They needed to stop the fire, and they needed to do it as soon as possible.

The problem was that they couldn't step away from this dragon in case they were planning on doing even more damage.

Merrick grunted and pushed Arlen away, but Arlen stood his ground. They both looked up when they heard the sirens of the fire trucks rushing toward them, and the other dragon took the chance to jump up. They extended both their wings, and while one of them was slightly bent, it held the dragon's weight. They flew up toward the ceiling, and before Arlen could do anything, they crashed through it and into the sky.

No matter how much he wanted to, Arlen didn't try going after the dragon. Instead, he pushed Merrick toward the exit. Merrick was limping just a bit, but they managed to reach the door, and they quickly shifted. They were naked, but there was no way out of it. They had to leave the club before the firefighters arrived.

Arlen wrapped an arm around Merrick's waist and helped him walk out. Smoke and fire billowed out of the club, illuminating the night. It broke Arlen's heart to see what was happening to his club, to the place where he'd poured in so much money and love.

He'd rebuild. He'd known something like this could happen when he decided to stay in town, close to the clan.

"Arlen!" a voice yelled.

Arlen turned to see Mallory and Baxter running toward them. He was relieved to have someone to help him with Merrick, and together, the three of them guided him toward an SUV parked by the sidewalk. Baxter quickly ran around it, opening the doors, then the trunk. Arlen helped Merrick lower himself into the backseat and finally took a good look at his best friend.

Just like there had been in his dragon form, there was blood on Merrick's face. A long cut ran from the corner of his eye to his mouth, and it was a miracle his eye was still intact. His skin was caked with soot and dirt, but he was in one piece, and that was all that mattered.

"Do I need to get you to a healer?" Arlen asked. His instinct was to do so without asking Merrick, but his friend wouldn't thank him for that.

Merrick shook his head. "I'll be fine."

"You're limping," Mallory pointed out.

"It's nothing. I put down my foot to avoid that dragon, and I didn't see the table. It's just a scratch."

Arlen crouched to make sure Merrick wasn't lying, and he was relieved to see that it truly was just a scratch. It would bruise, no doubt, and he needed to clean the scratch, but Merrick would be fine.

"There," Baxter said as he emerged from the trunk with a bunch of clothes bundled in his arms. "They might be too big or too small on you, but at least you won't be running around naked. The firefighters just arrived, and they're focused on the fire, but that won't last long. You should get dressed."

Arlen was happy to accept the clothes. He quickly put on a pair of jeans and a t-shirt, then shoved his feet into a pair of flip-flops Baxter found in the back of the SUV. He didn't care about being naked, but the firefighters would have questions about it if he was, and he couldn't afford to answer them.

Baxter was helping Merrick put on some clothes, so Arlen turned to Mallory. He was staring, and he stepped closer when he saw that Arlen was done dressing. "Are you hurt?" he asked.

Arlen shook his head. "I might be a bit bruised by tomorrow, but I'll be fine."

"Good, because the firefighters are coming this way."

Arlen turned and groaned when he saw Mallory wasn't lying. Two men dressed in the firefighter uniform strode toward them, and their expressions were grim.

"We were told you're the owner," one of them said.

Arlen nodded. "I am."

"Do you know what happened?"

Arlen couldn't exactly tell them that three dragons had fought in the middle of the club and set it on fire. Instead, he shook his head. "I don't. I was upstairs in my apartment, and I realized something was wrong only when my best friend and head of security came to get me." Arlen nodded in Merrick's direction. "We managed to get downstairs, but everything was already on fire by the time we did. Did everyone get out?" Arlen already knew that was true, but he had to behave as if he didn't.

"From what we could see. The bouncers and bartenders said they'd made sure everyone got out, but we'll have to check once the fire is out."

Arlen was getting a headache, and he wanted nothing more than to crawl into his bed and sleep for a week, but there was a problem.

His bed had burned down.

He and Merrick both had lived above the club. The apartment had been tiny, but they hadn't needed much space. Their entire lives had been there, though, and now, they'd burned down, along with the club. They'd have to start from the beginning again, and Arlen prayed he'd have the strength to do so.

Once the firefighters left, Mallory moved closer again. Without asking, he wrapped an arm around Arlen's waist. He kept his hold loose so that Arlen could step away if he wanted, but instead, Arlen leaned against Mallory's side. It was an odd position, since he was at least five inches taller than Mallory, but he felt safe. He was tired, and Mallory would protect him if anyone else tried attacking him.

But they wouldn't. The clan had done enough damage for

one night, and they were no doubt celebrating ruining Arlen and Merrick's life. They couldn't imagine that they hadn't and that Arlen would rebuild everything they had burned down, even if it killed him.

CHAPTER FOUR

Even though Arlen was safe, Mallory was very much aware that he could have lost him. How could he not be? He'd been there, had seen the club collapse and the fire eating it. Everything Arlen and Merrick owned had been between those walls, including their private lives. They'd even lost the clothes on their backs when they shifted, and they had nowhere to go. That was why Baxter and Mallory had brought them back to the pack, and Mallory was glad they'd found Kieran already awake so they could tell him what had happened. He'd agreed to let the dragons stay with them, and while Mallory was glad for that, he couldn't help but wonder how it would complicate things.

The pack was already unhappy with the presence of so many vampires. What would they think about having dragon shifters here, too? Especially considering the dragons were the reason the vampires were here. This wasn't going to end well, but there hadn't been an alternative early this morning, so they'd done what they could.

But Mallory couldn't stop thinking about what he'd seen or how easily he could have lost Arlen before anything could have happened between them. They'd shared that kiss on the dance floor, but it wasn't enough. And what if Arlen had died? What if Mallory hadn't gotten a second chance with him?

Mallory sat up in his bed. He'd been awake a few hours already, but the sun had still been shining outside. He'd stayed in bed, listened to how quiet the house was, and had

58

obsessed over the fire and how much he could have lost. He was done with that. He knew what he had to do, and he intended to do it.

He hopped out of bed and headed to the bathroom. When he opened his bedroom door, he paused, listening to ensure no one else was in there. The house was still silent, so he made his way to the shower. He'd taken one when they'd come home, but he could still *feel* the smell of smoke on his skin and hair. He wasn't sure if it was an impression or if he actually smelled like it, but if he was going to talk to Arlen, he didn't want to remind him of what had happened.

Of course, there was no way Arlen would forget the fire. He'd lost his entire life, and he'd have to rebuild it from the ground.

The thought gave Mallory pause. Maybe it wasn't the best moment to talk to Arlen. Arlen had other things to focus on, including the war with the clan. But, on the other hand, maybe he also needed a distraction.

Mallory groaned, rubbed the water from his face, then grabbed the shampoo. He'd just talk to Arlen and see what the dragon said. Even after what had happened yesterday, Arlen could make his own decisions.

When he got out of the bathroom, Gladys was leaning against the wall, waiting for her turn. She gave him a sleepy smile, then disappeared inside while Mallory headed to his bedroom. He was already dressed, but he was nervous, and he checked his reflection in the mirror one last time. Maybe he really should wait. Would Arlen even be awake already? He led a nocturnal life, almost as if he were a vampire, but last night had been anything but normal. He probably needed rest.

And Mallory needed to stop obsessing over this.

He headed out of his bedroom again, this time in the direction of the bedroom where Arlen and Merrick were staying.

Merrick had insisted they share a bedroom, probably because he wanted to make sure Arlen was safe. Mallory was glad Arlen hadn't been alone last night, even though he'd kind of wanted to be the one to protect him.

When he reached their door, he knocked lightly. He didn't want to wake up anyone if they were still sleeping, but he was relieved when the door swung open a few seconds later.

The problem was that it wasn't the dragon he was looking for who'd answered.

Merrick glared down at him, not looking very awake. "What do you want?"

"I just wanted to check up on you."

Merrick grunted. He was wearing a pair of sweatpants and a t-shirt, both borrowed from the pack. Apparently, they had an infinite supply of sweatpants, t-shirts, and flip-flops. Mallory supposed it made sense since they were shifters.

"We're fine. I'm going to the kitchen to get coffee, and you and Arlen can talk. Don't have sex on my bed."

Merrick pushed past Mallory. Mallory watched him walk down the hallway toward the stairs. Merrick had been grumpy before, and Mallory wasn't surprised to see he was even grumpier now.

"Good evening," Arlen said from inside the bedroom.

Mallory's attention quickly went back to him. He had what he'd wanted—Arlen on his own so they could talk. He still wasn't sure this was the best idea, but maybe giving Arlen something else to focus on would help him. Besides, Arlen had seemed interested when they danced.

Mallory took a hesitant step into the bedroom. "Good evening. How are you feeling?"

Arlen was sitting on the edge of one of the beds, probably the one where he'd slept. He was putting on socks, but he paused and looked up at Mallory.

"Well, I've been better," he said.

He'd showered yesterday, too, and had gone to bed with his hair damp. Tonight, it was all over the place, sticking up around his face and making him look adorable. Mallory wanted nothing more than to go to him and smooth his hair down, but instead, he stood in the middle of the bedroom, awkwardly shuffling his feet.

"I'm sorry you lost the club and everything else," he murmured.

Arlen nodded. "Thank you. I'm sorry I lost them, too, but I'm not giving up."

"I didn't think you would. And I wanted you to know that I'll be there for you, whatever you need."

Arlen stared at Mallory for a moment. Mallory couldn't tell what he was thinking, but he desperately wanted to know.

"Thank you. Does what happened change things between us?"

Mallory was relieved that Arlen had been the one to bring it up. "Not on my side. I still want to explore what was happening on the dance floor before the fight. But I'll understand if you're too overwhelmed and busy for me. This is probably the worst moment to start a relationship."

But instead of agreeing, Arlen grinned. "Is that what we have? A relationship?"

Arlen left Mallory feeling like he wasn't quite sure of anything. It was an odd sensation, kind of unpleasant, but there was an easy way to get out of it.

Mallory closed the door behind himself, but he stayed in the middle of the room. He didn't want to sit on Merrick's bed or crowd Arlen.

"As I was saying, this is probably the worst moment to focus on your personal life, but I can't stop thinking about you," he confessed. "The team and I are here for the foreseeable future, and it looks like we might share a home, at least for a while. I don't want things to be awkward between us, but I'd like to see what could have happened if the fire hadn't destroyed everything. I just don't want to push you, especially considering everything that's been happening."

Arlen got to his feet. "Good. I thought I was the only one who felt that way."

"How could I not want more with you? You're everything."

Arlen stopped in front of Mallory. "I don't know about that, but I do know that you're the only thing I didn't lose last night." He grabbed Mallory's face with both his hands and leaned down. Mallory's body moved almost on its own, and Mallory found himself wrapped around Arlen and kissing him.

It wasn't like the kiss they'd shared last night. It was softer, more hesitant, as if they were both afraid the other would break. It was logical for Mallory to feel that way about Arlen, but why did Arlen feel like that?

"I'm not going anywhere," Mallory told him in a whisper.

"Good, because I don't think I could stand losing something else."

"You won't lose me or anyone else. I realize you barely know us, but we're here to help, and we will."

Arlen's gaze was intense as he stared at Mallory. "I'm glad for that, but it's not what I want to talk about right now." He leaned closer again, and Mallory smiled in anticipation of the next kiss they would share.

A knock on the door interrupted them. "They want to see us all downstairs for a meeting," Merrick's gruff voice announced. "So put your clothes back on."

Mallory sighed heavily, but Arlen was laughing. Mallory supposed he didn't mind being interrupted if it made Arlen laugh, although he hoped Merrick wouldn't make a habit of it.

Arlen would have rather stayed in his bedroom, kissing Mallory, but he was glad they weren't going to avoid talking about the fire. Yes, it hurt to have lost everything, but Arlen was already thinking about future plans. He wouldn't let the clan beat him down. He hadn't done that when he still lived with them, and he wouldn't start now.

He and Mallory walked downstairs holding hands. That was new for Arlen, and he kept peeking at Mallory, expecting him to take his hand away when they reached the others. They could hear the sound of the TV in the living room, and Mallory pulled Arlen that way.

Arlen hadn't seen much of the house when they'd arrived early this morning. He'd been given a quick tour so he could find what he needed. Then he'd grabbed a shower and had fallen into bed. He felt better now that he'd slept, and instead of sadness, anger and indignance were fueling him.

They walked into the living room, still holding hands. Arlen expected someone to say something, but they barely gave them a second glance. Merrick was already there, and while he gave a little snort at the sight, he also handed Arlen a steaming cup of coffee.

"I made enough for both of us," he said.

"Nothing for me?" Mallory asked, clearly teasing.

"I didn't know if you'd want to add blood to it or whatever."

Mallory wrinkled his nose. "God, no. Blood and coffee? That's disgusting."

Arlen wouldn't know, but he handed Mallory the cup after taking a sip of his coffee. Mallory looked surprised, but he took it and drank. It was doctored the way Arlen liked it, with a lot of sugar and cream. Mallory seemed to like it, or at the very least, he didn't have anything to say about it.

The TV caught Arlen's attention. A picture on the screen

showed him at some party a while ago. Then the picture vanished, and the burned-up club appeared.

It broke Arlen's heart to see it that way. Even when he'd first found the building, it hadn't been this bad. Now, just a few walls were still standing. The club was nothing more than a pile of burned trash and soot.

"How are you?" a man who'd been introduced to Arlen as Oren asked.

"Physically, Merrick and I are both fine," Arlen told him. "But we're angry."

Oren nodded. He looked relaxed in jeans and a t-shirt, but Arlen knew he was the team leader. Just like everyone else in the room, he was deadly when he wanted to be. "Understandable, and we'll help you in your fight with the clan."

"And how are you going to do that?" Merrick asked rather rudely.

Arlen was used the way Merrick talked, but these people weren't, and he didn't want to look like he and Merrick didn't appreciate what they were doing for them.

He cleared his throat. "I was wondering the same thing," he said more gently. "Not that I don't appreciate your help, but Merrick and I know the clan. Even with the entire wolf pack behind you, there's little you'll be able to do. They managed to burn down the club, even though Merrick and I are dragons."

Oren didn't seem angry or surprised by Arlen's words. "I agree that as it is, we won't be able to do much. We certainly don't have the entire pack behind us, since some members aren't happy about our presence here. We've been thinking," he said, gesturing at the people in the room. "And so far, the only way we can see to make this work is to find allies."

Arlen nodded. "I agree."

"So, will you and Merrick work with us?"

Merrick gave a little grunt, which Arlen translated. "We

want the clan to pay for what they've done to both of us, so yes, we'll ally with you." Besides, there was also Mallory. Arlen wanted to spend as much time as possible with him. Mallory was a conclave enforcer, and eventually, he'd have to go back to his life. In the meantime, he was Arlen's.

"We could use more information about the dragons."

Arlen leaned his hip against the back of the couch. "We can give you all the details we remember, but the main thing you have to know is that the clan is rich and unafraid of getting their hands dirty. To get what they want, they won't hesitate to kill, which is why we need to be extremely careful. I'd suggest not going anywhere on your own."

"Do they know about us?" one of the women asked.

"Even if they don't, you're vampires. They don't like vampires." They'd tried to create a war between the vampires and the dhampirs, and when that hadn't worked, they attempted to get the wolves and the vampires to kill each other.

"They don't like anyone but dragons, and not even all of them," Merrick said, pointing at himself and Arlen.

"Well, we don't have to get them to like us," Baxter pointed out.

Arlen wasn't surprised to find him here already, even though he didn't live here. He kept peeking at Mallory and Arlen, and he couldn't seem to stop smiling.

"Look, the clan doesn't like anyone but themselves," he explained. "And what they want is to have control over the entire town. They don't want other supernatural creatures to live here and possibly try to stop their drug dealing and other criminal endeavors, which means they'll do everything they can to get rid of all of us. It's why they targeted the pack. They see the pack as a powerful entity that could stop them in their conquest."

"So what we need is people who'll help us fight them," Oren said.

Arlen nodded. "I can call several people. I met many different supernatural creatures through the club, and most of them disliked the clan. I don't know if everyone will want to help or will be able to, but I can ask. Reaching out won't cost me anything." Luckily, Arlen's contacts and most of the stuff he'd had on his phone were uploaded to the cloud.

"And I could call my family," Mallory said.

That brought everyone's attention to him. Arlen wasn't sure what Mallory's family had to do with this, but the members of Mallory's team seemed excited.

"You think your sister will come?" the same woman as before—Arlen *really* had to learn their names—asked.

Mallory rolled his eyes. "I don't see why not. You know how much they all love a good fight."

Oren was already nodding. "If you think they'll want to be involved, call them. We can use all the help we can find."

"Well, you know you'll get a lot of help with them."

Arlen was more curious than ever. He and Mallory hadn't yet talked about much, but he wanted to find out everything there was to know about the vampire. It seemed his family was a good first step, although it puzzled Arlen. Surely, Mallory had been a vampire for a while. That would mean his family had died some time ago. "You think they'll help?" he asked.

Mallory smiled at him. "They definitely will. I texted them about what happened, and several of them have already declared they're coming to me."

"Several of them?" Merrick asked, sounding as if he dreaded the answer his question would bring.

"All eight of them. Well, nine if you include our creator."

That made more sense. "You're not related by blood," Arlen said.

"No. We're not related at all, unless you agree that our creator is our father. We've always been close, though."

They had to be if they were all ready to step in and fight for Mallory. It was a surprise because, as far as Arlen knew, vampires created by the same person didn't have a reason to stay together. Sometimes they made up a coven, but more often than not, after a while, they drifted apart. It was how things went when people were immortal, Arlen supposed.

Finding out that Mallory was close to his vampire family made him like Mallory even more.

"I know I'm going to regret it, but please, tell all of them to come if they can," Oren said.

"Regret it?" Merrick asked.

"They can be a lot," Mallory explained. "I mean, just the fact that there are nine of them means that their presence is always a bit of a mess. When we're all together, we're noisy and occupy a lot of space. But you won't find anyone more loyal to you and your cause. If you need someone to watch your back during a fight, they'll do it. You can trust them with your life. I know I do."

Arlen was more than ever curious to meet all these people, so he was glad when Mallory agreed to call them after they finished talking. He was discovering a lot about Mallory, and while it wasn't quite the way he'd imagined, he supposed it could have been worse.

He or Mallory could have died in the fire, and then they wouldn't have had the opportunity of getting to know each other. They wouldn't have had the opportunity of doing anything.

"So, your family," Arlen said.

Mallory found himself smiling. He always did when his family was involved.

They were a lot to deal with, but Mallory was used to it. Besides, the fact that they didn't all live in the same city helped. They seldom gathered all together, and when they did, it was a party. It never lasted long, and it was enough to keep Mallory going for months after that.

He loved all of them, even the ones who annoyed him the most, and like every single one of them, he'd be there in a heartbeat if any of them needed him.

"You love them," Arlen murmured, staring at Mallory.

"I do."

"Correct me if I'm wrong, but isn't that an oddity in the vampire world?"

Mallory nodded, because it was. He just had to think about his friends and team members to have proof of that. As far as he was aware, none of them were still in contact with the people who'd turned them into vampires. Vampires lived long lives, and after a while, they tended to drift away from each other—when they didn't try killing each other for whatever reason. It was odd, but from what Mallory had observed, vampires had the capacity of holding a grudge much longer than many of the other creatures he'd met. One would think that living forever, they'd forgive and forget, but maybe that was exactly why they couldn't. They had an enormous length of time to think about revenge.

"You're not wrong," he told Arlen. "As far as I know, most vampires don't stay in contact with their makers or the other vampires their makers created."

"Yet, you did."

"It probably has to do with the fact that we all lived together for a time. It truly was like a family."

"Can I ask a few questions?"

Mallory and Arlen had left the living room. A few people were still there, talking about their next steps, but they weren't solving any of their problems, and Mallory wanted to spend time with Arlen. He'd dragged him out here, and it felt like they were alone in the darkness of the porch. Mallory could still hear the voices from the living room, but it was easy enough to ignore them.

"Ask away," he told Arlen.

"Why did you become a vampire? Was it your choice?"

Mallory understood the question. Many times, maybe most times, vampires didn't choose to be turned. Even some members of Mallory's team had been forced into this life, and while they'd learned to live with it, it didn't make it right.

"I was sick," he said. "Cancer. I was going to die, and I was in so much pain that I kind of wanted it to happen. I only had my mother left, but she had dementia, and she wouldn't even recognize me when I managed to get out of bed to take care of her. I thought I was going to die before her, but instead, she managed to sneak out one night. I went after her as soon as I realized, but when I found her, she was dead. It was cold, and she'd been barefoot in her nightgown."

Mallory was startled when Arlen took his hand, even though the touch was gentle. Arlen didn't move away, but he did freeze, no doubt to give Mallory time to decide what he wanted. Since Mallory wanted Arlen to hold his hand, he twisted his and linked their fingers together. He gave a little squeeze, almost ashamed of how much emotion was in his voice.

"It happened so long ago that it probably shouldn't hurt the way it still does," he said with a chuckle.

"You lost your mother. I think it's always going to hurt, at least a bit. There's no shame in that."

"I know. I just don't talk about her often. My friends and family all know about her, and it's not something I tell strangers or people I'm not close to."

"You're not close to me. We only met a few nights ago."

"Yet, it feels like forever."

Arlen was silent for a moment. "I suppose it does. Do you want to continue or to stop talking?"

Mallory might as well get it out of the way. Besides, he wanted Arlen to know where he came from. "I don't know how long I sat there, holding her body. It was cold, and after a while, I became numb. I think that if Tynan hadn't found me, I would have let myself die. I was already unconscious, and I barely noticed it when he picked me up and carried me away. When I woke up, I didn't recognize the place where I was. I freaked out, but Tynan was there. He told me what happened, and he said he was sorry for my mother's death, that he took care of her body, and that he'd take me to her grave as soon as I was better. I cried."

She was still buried there, in the small cemetery that belonged to Tynan's family, right next to Tynan's parents, siblings, and family.

Arlen's hand tightened around Mallory's. The pain was still there, but it had softened a long time ago.

"He told me who he was and what he was. He told me he could save me and explained what it would mean for me. At first, I said no. I just wanted to die because I didn't have anything else to live for. I got sick after spending so much time in the cold, and he took care of me, along with some of my siblings. They were the ones who convinced me to get turned. I healed from the illness I got that night, but I was still sick. Tynan was worried about me, and the next time he asked, I said yes."

"I'm glad you did. We wouldn't have met otherwise, and I can't think of a world without you in it."

Mallory leaned sideways, and he wasn't surprised when Arlen let go of his hand and wrapped his arms around his shoulders. "I'm glad I said yes, too. Even though I thought I might have made a mistake in the beginning, it opened a world of opportunities for me. I lost my mother, but I found a father figure and siblings."

"Were you the last your creator turned?"

"No. I was the fourth."

"I can assume that all of you were turned because you were ill?"

"Yes. Tynan would never turn someone against their will, and without a good reason. It's not the kind of vampire he is. He also doesn't turn someone very often. He wants to be sure everyone understands what they're in for if he does. He just wants to give more to people who didn't have opportunities when they were humans."

Sometimes Mallory wondered if what Tynan was doing was right. He'd never turned anyone himself, and he had no intention of doing so. But he didn't blame his father. Tynan was extremely old, and Mallory knew as well as every old vampire that sometimes, loneliness was too much. As long as Tynan made sure that everyone involved wanted to be turned, Mallory had no problem with it. Besides, it had given him his siblings, and they were everything to him.

He cleared his throat. "So, my siblings will come. Do you think you can get more people to help us?"

If Arlen was startled by the change in their conversation, he didn't say anything about it. "I know several leaders in the supernatural community in town. Not all of them frequented the club, but Merrick and I introduced ourselves when we first arrived. We wanted everyone to know that we weren't part of the clan even though we were dragon shifters. I don't know if all of them will be able to help us, but they'll certainly listen to us."

"Good. We'll need all the manpower we can get."

Arlen sighed. He pressed his cheek against Mallory's hair, and Mallory found himself snuggling against his side. He couldn't remember the last time he'd felt so soft and open. He didn't usually tell his life story to people he'd only met a few days before.

"I just hope we can pull enough people together."

Mallory hoped the same, but only the future would tell.

When they went back inside, Arlen noticed Merrick talking to Sloan. It reminded him of something, and instead of following Mallory upstairs like he wanted, he pulled Mallory toward them. Sloan seemed to be on his way out, but both he and Merrick looked up when they heard Arlen and Mallory.

"Do you think it would be a good idea to contact your creator's replacement?" he asked.

Sloan and Mallory were confused, but Merrick knew what Arlen was asking. Arlen wasn't surprised when he groaned. "Do I really have to? You know I don't like him."

"Yeah, but we need all the help we can find, and what better help than a vampire coven?"

"What are you talking about?" Mallory blurted out.

Arlen stared at Merrick. He wouldn't tell anyone his secret, although he was certainly pushing him to do so. He didn't fully understand why Merrick wouldn't tell these people about it. They were trustworthy, and they needed help.

Merrick glared, then rubbed the back of his head. "I was turned," he said.

"I don't understand." If anything, Mallory sounded even more confused now.

"I was born a dragon shifter, but an asshole decided he wanted to see what happened if he tried turning me into a vampire."

Mallory's jaw just about hit the floor. "Is that even possible?"

"You tell me. I'm standing here in front of you, aren't I?"

"But you're a dragon shifter."

"With a bit of a bite now. I can eat food, but I can also drink blood. I just can't survive on it because my dragon needs more energy. I can also walk in the sun, although I burn easily."

Mallory seemed to have trouble digesting this. "I didn't think it was possible. What happened to your creator?"

"I killed him. I don't have any contact with his coven or with any vampire."

"You do now," Arlen intervened. "And I think you should contact Harmon's coven, at the very least, to tell him what the clan is doing. He might lose coven members to this drug."

"Fine. I'll call him. You know he'll want to be involved, though. He always wants to be involved when I am."

Arlen suspected it was because they were kind of brothers, having been turned into vampires by the same man. As far as he knew, Harmon didn't have anyone else, and while he led a coven, it wasn't exactly a family. Arlen had tried to make Merrick see that, but Merrick didn't want anything to do with his creator, and that included the other vampires the man had created.

"Well, I'm headed home," Sloan declared. "Baxter and I want to spend some time together before I go to bed."

"We're going to get some rest, too," Arlen told him with a smile.

"Mallory's a vampire. Should he stay awake?" Merrick asked.

Arlen glared at him, but from his best friend's smirk, he could tell Merrick was teasing him. He ignored him and pulled Mallory toward the stairs, ready to spend time alone with him. He'd earned it after everything that had happened, dammit.

"So Merrick is a vampire?" Mallory asked as they climbed the stairs.

"Yep."

"What does that mean for him? He mentioned being able to eat food and go in the sun, so it's clear the vampire side isn't strong, but it's so weird that it's there at all."

Arlen hummed and continued dragging Mallory along. He

went straight to Mallory's room since he shared with Merrick, or at least, he'd shared with him until he and Mallory had gotten together.

Mallory was still asking questions about Merrick, but Arlen didn't have answers for him. He grinned when he pushed open the door of Mallory's room, hauled Mallory inside, and slammed the door shut. Then he pressed Mallory against it and looked down at him.

"You'll have to ask Merrick about all of this, but do you really want to do it now?" he drawled.

Mallory snapped his mouth shut and swallowed. He shook his head, and since he was silent now, Arlen leaned down and kissed him. They were alone, and while there were other people in the house, Arlen didn't care. He finally had Mallory all to himself, and he wouldn't waste the opportunity.

He pulled away from the door, taking Mallory with him. They didn't stop kissing, even though they stumbled. He had to look up to make sure they'd reached the bed, and when he saw they had, he pushed Mallory onto it. Mallory's pupils were blown, and the tip of his fangs poked from under his upper lip. His cheeks were just the slightest bit flushed, and he was the most beautiful thing Arlen had ever seen.

"What do you want?" he asked.

"Everything." Mallory sounded breathless.

Arlen wanted to give him everything, but this was the first time they were having sex, and he didn't want it to be overwhelming. It kind of was for him, and he couldn't imagine things were different for Mallory. They had eternity to do whatever they could think of. The need to have all of it right now was there, but Arlen also wanted to take his time.

First things first, though. He needed to get Mallory naked.

He reached down and took off Mallory's shoes. Mallory jerked up and tugged on his t-shirt, and together, they got him naked. Arlen threw the clothes behind himself, more focused on what was in front of him than on what happened to them.

"Beautiful," he breathed out when Mallory reclined back on the bed, fully exposed. The hair on his chest was slightly darker than the blond hair on his head, and it created a line that went down the middle of his stomach, straight to his erect cock. The curly hair at its base was trimmed, but Arlen wouldn't have cared if it hadn't been.

Mallory shook his head. "Not like you."

He wasn't trying to hide his body, for which Arlen was glad. There was nothing he needed to hide, not even the scars on his chest and sides. Mallory was a fighter, and it showed on his body.

"I'm nothing special," Arlen said.

Since Mallory was naked, it was Arlen's turn. He tugged off his t-shirt. Mallory didn't help him, seemingly happy to watch him, which was perfectly fine with him. Arlen didn't have a problem with nudity. He was naked every time he shifted.

But once they were both naked, Arlen didn't know where to start. He understood why Mallory had said he wanted everything, and he wanted the same, but it was overwhelming. Mallory seemed to understand that, and he opened his arms.

Arlen was relieved. He dropped between them, and Mallory wrapped them around him. They kissed again, and while the urgency they'd felt before was still there, simmering under the surface, it was nice to slow things down and feel Mallory against him.

Arlen rubbed his hands over Mallory's body, feeling the dips and mounds, the rougher areas, the scars. Mallory's hair prickled Arlen's palms, and he could feel Mallory's muscles bunch and release under his touch.

Arlen needed more, so he tore himself away from Mallory's lips and kissed down Mallory's neck. Mallory tilted his head to give Arlen better access, and Arlen took advantage of that. He explored Mallory's neck, the spaces just under his ears, then behind them. Kissing and gently biting Mallory there made Mallory shudder, so Arlen repeated the gesture while caressing down Mallory's chest and stomach until he reached Mallory's cock. He wrapped his fingers around it, smiling at how hard it was. Mallory wanted him as much as he wanted Mallory.

He was touching Arlen as much as Arlen was touching him, and Arlen found himself thrusting forward when Mallory cupped his ass with both his hands. There was a wicked glint in Mallory's gaze now, and his touch became more certain and insistent. He was exploring Arlen's body like Arlen was exploring his, and Arlen was perfectly fine to continue doing this. He wanted more, but this was good, too.

He returned his lips to Mallory's mouth. His tongue scraped against Mallory's fang, the pain barely there, but for some reason, Mallory groaned. Arlen realized Mallory could taste his blood and that he liked it. He pushed their bodies closer together, let go of Mallory's cock, and plastered himself against him. His cock rubbed against Mallory's, but that wasn't what Arlen was focused on.

He pressed the tip of his tongue harder against Mallory's fang. Mallory kissed him deeper, swiping his tongue against Arlen's to lick the few drops of blood that had beaded there. Arlen had never realized that drinking someone's blood could be erotic for vampires, but the discovery delighted him. He didn't mind losing a little blood if it gave Mallory pleasure.

"What do you need?" he asked, his voice little more than a growl.

"This. This is — it's perfect." Mallory sounded as rough as Arlen felt.

As if to show him how perfect it was for him, Mallory wrapped his legs around Arlen's hips. His thighs were thick and strong and hairy, and feeling anchored like that in Mallory's arms was almost better than feeling Mallory move against him. Sex was similar with everyone—two people, mostly naked, taking their pleasure—but Arlen's feelings for Mallory made it the best sex of Arlen's life. He couldn't have wanted anything more.

He had everything he needed in his arms.

He kissed Mallory harder, the movements of his tongue mirroring the rhythm of his hips. Mallory caught it and sucked on the tip, drawing more blood from it. He was taking what he needed, and Arlen loved it, especially when one of Mallory's hands slipped into his hair and held him in place. He scraped his tongue against Mallory's fang again, and more blood appeared. Mallory lapped that up, too, shuddering and moaning as his cock jerked against Arlen's stomach.

This was all Arlen wanted, and he lost himself in the sounds Mallory made, in the smell of their bodies, of sex and blood. The pleasure he felt reached a tipping point, and for one second, he hovered there.

Then he fell, and Mallory caught him.

Arlen cried out and had to stop kissing Mallory to breathe through the pleasure coursing through his body. He pressed their foreheads together and focused on Mallory. He wanted to feel him come and shudder in his arms, and that was what he got. He held Mallory through it the way Mallory had held him, gently twisting them to the side so he wouldn't get too heavy. Mallory didn't seem to care. He buried his face against Arlen's neck, not to bite him, just to breathe him in and relax.

Arlen pressed his nose to Mallory's hair inhaling his scent. He almost couldn't believe that he really had this, and he'd do whatever he had to in order to never lose it.

They stayed silent for a moment, and Arlen reveled in their closeness.

"So, tell me more about Merrick being a vampire," Mallory

eventually said.

Arlen laughed. "That's what you want to talk about while we're naked in bed?"

Mallory propped himself up on an elbow and looked down at Arlen. "Or we could have sex again."

It would take Arlen a moment to be ready to go again, but he wouldn't mind trying to get there sooner. He hooked an arm around Mallory's neck and pulled him down, cutting off the laughter coming from Mallory with his mouth.

Yes, they could try this again.

CHAPTER FIVE

They hadn't officially moved in together, but Arlen had been spending every night with Mallory, and Mallory couldn't have been happier. They didn't need to talk about things to know where they stood. They were just together, and with all the work everyone was doing, Mallory was happy that he got to go to bed with Arlen every evening. They didn't always have sex, but they didn't need to. Being wrapped around each other and falling asleep that way was more than good enough and just as satisfying.

Okay, maybe it wasn't as satisfying, but Mallory wouldn't change any of this for all the gold in the world.

But it made him think. Once this mess with the dragons was over, what would happen? He couldn't go back to the conclave, even if the conclave suddenly turned into a tolerant group of people who wanted to help everyone and not just vampires. He was done with that, at least for the next few decades. Instead, he wanted to stay here in town, live with Arlen, and be close to Robin and Baxter. Even Kieran and Sloan were starting to grow on him, and he wanted to get to know them better.

The problem was the pack. Most of them were still wary, and Mallory hoped that in time, they'd realize no one was going to attack them to suck their blood while they were walking in the forest. Some pack members were outright aggressive, though, and Mallory believed that eventually, something would break. No one was happy about the situation, but this was on the wolves' shoulders, not on his or his team's.

"You're already thinking too hard," Arlen murmured from his side of the bed.

Mallory hadn't wanted to wake him up, but now that Arlen was awake, he rolled toward him. Arlen greeted him with a smile and open arms, and Mallory snuggled between them. "Sorry. I just didn't want to wake you up, and I wasn't sure what else to do other than think."

Arlen kissed Mallory's forehead. "One day, this will explode, and what will I do then?"

"You'll find someone to replace me."

"But I don't want to replace you. I want you to live forever and to forever be in my bed."

"I'm sure we can find a way to make that work," Mallory murmured as he kissed Arlen's jaw.

They were under the blankets, warm and comfortable, and Mallory didn't want to get up. Reality awaited them outside of their nest, something Mallory wasn't ready to deal with yet. He was more than happy to delay it, especially when the main reason for that delay was naked in his arms.

The door slammed open. Mallory jerked into a sitting position, trying to scramble out of the blankets. If they were under attack, he'd defend Arlen, even if it meant he'd die.

"Oh my god!" someone screeched. "Brain bleach! I need brain bleach. I saw Mallory naked."

Mallory groaned and quickly dove back under the blankets. He pulled them around his waist, ensuring that not one inch of offending flesh was on display. Then he turned to Arlen, who was still sitting next to him, looking puzzled. He was mostly covered, too, so Mallory could turn his attention to the intruder.

"What are you doing here?" he asked his brother, Alpin.

Alpin had pressed both hands to his face, but he opened his fingers to peek at Mallory. Mallory glared, but he gestured at the blankets around his waist so that Alpin would know it was safe for him to look.

Alpin dropped his hands and grinned. "I was told to wake you up."

"And you had to do it like this?"

"I didn't think you'd be in bed with this delicious man," Alpin said.

His gaze drifted over to Arlen, and Mallory snapped his fingers to get his brother's attention back. "Does your presence here mean that everyone has arrived?" Mallory hadn't realized it was that late.

"I don't know about everyone. I just saw Dad."

"And who told you to come and wake me up?"

"That delicious piece of man you call leader."

"That would be Oren, and he's involved with someone, so keep your hands off him."

Alpin pouted. "Is there anyone who isn't involved around here? I'm gonna need my daily dose of sex if I have to fight a dragon."

Arlen made a sound that Mallory was pretty sure was a muffled laugh. He wanted to strangle his brother, but he supposed Arlen would have to meet all of them soon, anyway. Alpin was probably the worst brother to meet, though, especially as the first one.

"I don't know about the wolves, but all the guys on my team are in relationships." He didn't mention Renata or Gladys, since Alpin was gay. "There's also Merrick, but I'm pretty sure he'd rather tear your head off than date you."

Alpin waved Mallory's words away. "Who said anything about dating? I just mentioned sex."

Mallory groaned. Alpin was going to be the death of him. He probably already would have been, if Mallory could die. "Why don't you head downstairs? Arlen and I will get dressed and join you as soon as possible."

Alpin wiggled his eyebrows. "Yeah? Or are you going to

stay in bed for a while longer? I have to say, if your boyfriend were with anyone else, I'd ask if I could watch." He shuddered in horror. "But since you're the only other naked guy here, my answer is no."

"No one asked you to stay and watch anything. Can you leave?"

Alpin gave Mallory a little salute and finally turned toward the door. "It was a pleasure meeting you, Arlen. I'll see you downstairs."

Arlen's laughter wasn't muffled anymore. He was laughing outright, and Mallory found himself smiling.

"I love my brother, but he can be a lot."

Arlen hiccupped. "I can see that. Is he always like that?"

"Pretty much. He's the youngest, and he's still sowing his wild oats."

"He's cute."

Mallory narrowed his eyes, but he couldn't deny it was true. Alpin's curly blond hair and blue eyes made him look like a cherub, and as long as he didn't open his mouth, people thought he was a little angel. Then he either insulted them or propositioned them, and they realized he was a horny asshole. "Maybe you picked the wrong brother."

Arlen hooked an arm around Mallory's neck. "I think I picked the perfect brother."

They kissed, and Mallory wished he could stay here for the rest of the night. Unfortunately, he could hear Alpin talking to someone, and he knew he needed to step in before whoever it was tried to kill him. His team knew to ignore Alpin, but the wolves wouldn't be nice to him if he pushed them. Sometimes, Alpin didn't realize it would be better for him to keep his mouth shut.

With a groan, Mallory pushed away from Arlen. "We should head downstairs."

"I wish we didn't have to."

"You're not the only one, but I'm pretty sure it wouldn't take much for Merrick to want to strangle Alpin, and I quite like my brother, even though he can be annoying."

"You love him."

Mallory sighed. "Unfortunately for me."

But no matter how playful Alpin was, if he had to fight for one of their siblings, he would. He was fierce and could be serious when the situation required it, although Mallory couldn't remember the last time he'd seen Alpin serious.

"Come on," Arlen said as he got out of bed. "I want to meet your family."

And Mallory wanted them to meet Arlen, but he couldn't look away from Arlen's long body. He was gorgeous, and Mallory would never tire of watching him move casually, as if he weren't naked. Mallory didn't have a problem with nakedness, and he wasn't ashamed of his body, but he wasn't as comfortable as Arlen. He supposed it had to do with Arlen being a shifter and needing to be naked often enough that it was one of his natural states.

Mallory was eager to learn every single thing that made Arlen different, but right now, he didn't have time.

He needed to face his family.

Arlen couldn't remember the last time he'd had so much fun. Not that the situation with the clan and the pack was fun, but being with Mallory and his friends, and now, his family? He loved it. He'd only met one of Mallory's brothers for now, and only briefly, but he could already tell he was going to love Alpin.

He suspected Merrick wouldn't. Alpin was Merrick's opposite, and unless Arlen was mistaken, they were going to clash.

He and Merrick had gone shopping, so they each had a car,

a phone, and new clothes. Arlen was grateful for what the pack had done for him and what they'd given him, but he was glad he didn't have to borrow clothes anymore. Kieran insisted that they didn't belong to anyone, and Arlen could understand that, but he still felt better wearing his personal jeans and shirt.

He and Mallory took turns in the bathroom. Mallory was waiting for Arlen when Arlen left the room, and he held out his hand for Arlen to take. Arlen did. It looked like Mallory wasn't going to hide the fact that they were together, although Arlen supposed it would've been hard, since one of Mallory's brothers had walked in on them in bed this morning. But Mallory was relaxed as they walked down the stairs and toward the kitchen, where the voices came from.

The kitchen wasn't a small room, but it appeared small this evening, with so many people stuffed inside. Baxter was sitting at the counter, his hands wrapped around a stainless-steel mug. His gaze bounced from one person in the room to another, never stopping. Robin was next to him, but Kieran and Sloan were on their feet, and both they and Merrick were drinking coffee, from the smell of it.

Arlen made a beeline for the coffee pot. He had to push a few people out of his way to get to it, but he did so with an apology, and they didn't argue or point out his rudeness. He felt better once he had his own cup clutched in hand. It gave him something to focus on, a buffer between him and Mallory's family.

Arlen was happy to meet them and extremely curious, but he'd never done this *meeting the family* thing, and he wasn't sure what to expect. He wanted them to like him, and he wasn't sure how to make that happen.

"You look as good wrapped in clothing as you did naked," Alpin said with a waggle of his eyebrows. He was sitting on the counter, and he, too, was sipping on what had to be blood.

"So he's Mallory's boyfriend?" a woman asked. She was leaning against the wall, with another woman Arlen didn't recognize, and Renata next to her. The three had been talking until Alpin opened his mouth.

Mallory groaned loudly enough to get everyone's attention. "Okay, let's get this out of the way so everyone knows everyone. This is Arlen, and yes, he's my boyfriend. He's also a dragon shifter. The grumpy-looking man at the table drinking coffee is his best friend, Merrick. He's half-dragon shifter, half-vampire." Or something like that. Mallory still wasn't sure how it worked.

Alpin's eyes widened, and he hopped off the counter. "Really? I've never met anyone who was a mixed breed like that. Do you bite people for blood?"

Merrick glared at Alpin, and Arlen could have sworn he snarled when Alpin came closer and flopped into one of the empty chairs.

Mallory gestured at Arlen to come to him, and Arlen did. He suspected it had something with the dignified gentleman standing next to Mallory. He'd seen them hug while he'd been pouring his coffee, and he wondered who it was.

"Dad, this is Arlen. Arlen, this is my father, Tynan."

When Tynan offered Arlen his hand, Arlen shook it. He had no interest in anyone but Mallory, but he couldn't deny Tynan was handsome. He seemed to be in his late thirties, possibly early forties, although that didn't mean anything for a vampire. His piercing blue eyes stared at Arlen as if he were trying to read him, but a smile played on his full lips. His beard and mustache were short and neatly cut, just like his brown hair. It had a bit of a curl, just enough to look a bit messy but still elegant.

"It's a pleasure to meet you, Arlen," Tynan said. His voice was deep and smooth.

"The same goes for me." And it really was, although Arlen

wished they'd met in different circumstances.

Mallory turned toward the rest of the room. "For everyone who doesn't know them, these are Sloan and Kieran. They're respectively the beta and the alpha of this pack, and they agreed to house the bunch of you, even though I told them it wasn't necessary and that you could find a hotel."

"A hotel?" one of Mallory's brothers asked. "You'd put us up in a hotel?"

"I'd put you up anywhere if it meant I didn't have to deal with you on a daily basis."

The man didn't look offended. Instead, he snorted and strode toward Mallory and pulled him into his arms. Mallory went easily, and there was a bit of backslapping before the brothers stepped away from each other.

Mallory turned back to Arlen. "This is Rex." He continued pointing at the people in the room that Arlen didn't recognize. "These are Yvonne, Meyer, Parker, Umberto, Magda, Cressida, and you already know Alpin."

Arlen's mind spun with the new names. He'd barely learned the names of the people in Mallory's team, and now there were a bunch of new ones.

"Of course, I'm the best brother," Alpin said. He was staring at Merrick as he did so. "You'll find out soon enough."

Arlen was pretty sure he was joking, but since Alpin was focused on Merrick, he'd let his friend deal with the vampire. He had enough other people to deal with.

A yell coming from outside the house made all of them jump. It was easy to recognize who was a conclave member and who wasn't by everyone's reaction. Mallory and his team members were on their feet right away, rushing toward the front of the house. Mallory's family was slower, but from the way they moved, still efficient. They probably had some kind of fighting experience, which was a relief, because it was what they needed to fight the clan.

But this evening, it wasn't the clan they had to fight. It wasn't dragons they found standing in front of the house when they stepped onto the porch, making it groan from the number of people there. Arlen only had enough time to wonder if the porch would hold them all before he noticed the group of people standing in front of it.

The night was dark, but he didn't have a problem seeing them. He suspected they were all wolves, from what he could smell, which meant they probably belonged to the pack. It was why everyone stayed back except for Kieran and Sloan, who stepped off the porch and moved toward the group.

A woman stepped forward. "You brought even more vampires into our pack," she accused.

Kieran looked both tired and angry. "I did."

"How could you? This is a pack, not a vampire coven. We won't allow them to turn us into bloodsuckers."

Alpin snorted loudly, then cupped a hand on his mouth. Merrick glared at him, but everyone else was more focused on the wolves. Were they going to attack? It didn't sound good, but Arlen didn't want to assume. He barely knew these people, and they'd been welcoming so far.

It looked like they might not be for much longer.

"What are you doing here?" Kieran asked as he looked around the group. His gaze stopped on the woman again.

"What do you think? We're taking back the pack."

"What are you talking about, Fay? The pack was never taken away from you, so there's nothing to take back."

"That's a lie. You're turning this pack into a coven, and we're done with it. You can't do this, Kieran. Vampires shouldn't be allowed to live with us, and they shouldn't be taking away resources from us."

"What resources?" Alpin asked. Once again, everyone turned to him. He didn't seem to care. Instead, he shrugged and continued, "I mean, we drink blood. Unless this is a special kind of pack, I don't think we're taking anything away from them."

He wasn't wrong, but unfortunately, his words made the woman—Fay—angrier. "You're invading us," she snapped. "And our alpha is helping you. We won't stand for that. You need to leave, and you need to do it now."

"I invited them here. You have no right to demand they go," Kieran said. His voice had gone low and menacing, so Arlen wasn't surprised to see a few of the wolves standing behind Fay take a step back.

She didn't. Instead, she stood there, staring at Kieran. "Either they go, or we do," she declared.

That wasn't what Mallory had expected, although he couldn't say he was sorry. He'd thought Fay and the people behind her would attack, but instead, it sounded like she was giving Kieran an ultimatum.

Those never went well.

"What do you mean?" Kieran asked.

He sounded wary, and Mallory didn't blame him. Fay might be his sister, but she hadn't been behaving very sisterly. Baxter had explained to Mallory and the rest of the team what had happened with Kieran's father, so Mallory wasn't surprised. From what Baxter had said, Fay had always been on their father's side.

"You pushed our father away to take his place as the alpha, but you've been pandering to vampires ever since. So either you order them to leave, or we go," she said, gesturing at the people behind her.

Several were nodding, clearly on board with Fay's plan, but a few others, especially those at the back, were looking around as if they hadn't expected this. Maybe they hadn't. Mallory knew a few shifters, so he was aware of the fact that they were more comfortable living in a pack, and of course, the bigger the pack was, the safer they were. Even if every single person behind Fay went with her, it wouldn't be a huge pack. They'd have a hard time defending themselves.

Then there was the problem of finding a new territory that wasn't already under another pack's rule. Mallory understood that Fay was annoyed, angry, and probably scared, but this wasn't the right way to go about this.

"You want to leave the pack?" Kieran asked.

"We will if you don't kick the vampires out."

"You don't understand. We need their help." Kieran hesitated, then stepped closer to Fay.

She stayed where she was, her expression stubborn, but the group of people behind her stepped away, as if they were afraid he'd hurt them.

Mallory didn't know Kieran well, but the man was a good alpha, from what he'd seen. He'd never hurt a pack member without reason, so their reaction told Mallory that his father possibly had. The pack members were afraid of the alpha, even though he was new.

"We're dealing with a dragon clan," Kieran said. "They're the ones who've been killing vampires and dealing drugs. They want to get rid of the pack so they can have dominion over the town."

"They killed vampires, so they did a good thing as far as I'm concerned. Instead of allying with vampires, you could ally with them. They're shifters, even though they aren't wolves." Disgust dripped from Fay's voice every time she said the word *vampire*.

She seemed convinced that her plan was good, and Mallory supposed it would be if things were different, but they weren't. Both Kieran and Sloan were dating vampires, so there was no way they could ally with the dragons.

Kieran had to make a horrible decision, but he didn't have

a choice. Mallory's heart bled for him. He didn't know if he'd manage to choose between his family and the right thing to do.

He wasn't surprised when Kieran stood up straighter. His expression changed, and now, instead of being a pleading brother, he was a powerful alpha making decisions for the good of his pack.

"My alliance, the *pack's* alliance, is with the vampires," he declared, his voice loud enough that everyone around the house could hear him. "That won't change, because what the dragon clan is doing isn't right. You all have a choice. You can stay with the pack, get to know the vampires, and realize that they're no different than we are. They drink blood to survive, but they're not creatures of evil. The fight between our species has lasted for long enough, and it's time to realize that our ancestors were wrong. There are good and bad vampires, just like there are good and bad wolf shifters."

Kieran looked at his sister again, then addressed the whole group. "As the alpha, I've made decisions you might disagree with. You have to decide if you trust me, or if you'd rather go with Fay. If you do, we won't try to stop you. Take whatever you own, and leave. But you lose access to the homes you have here in pack territory. You also won't be welcome back, and if I find you in pack territory, I'll act accordingly. You'll be considered a different pack, and you'll have to follow the same rules and laws a different pack would. Think well about what you're doing. I won't take back anyone who leaves to-night."

Mallory sucked in a breath. Everyone, even the vampires, could tell it was a warning. Kieran was giving every pack member the opportunity to make their own choice, but they wouldn't be able to change their minds, not if they left. They wouldn't be pack members anymore, which meant they'd lose their home, possibly their family, and the pack's protection.

But that didn't seem to matter to Fay, who glared at her brother. "We don't care about any of that," she said. "You're ruining the pack, and we won't stand here and watch you while not doing anything. We'll create our own pack, and we'll thrive."

"And who will be your alpha?" Sloan asked. He looked angrier than Kieran, or maybe Kieran was just better at hiding his emotions. "You? Our father?"

"What do you care?"

"I don't. But I hope you remember that we won't take you back when you come back to us. This is a final decision, Fay, and it goes for all of you."

Sloan looked around the small group behind Fay. Mallory saw several of them stepping away, then disappearing into the forest. He suspected those wouldn't be going with Fay. Others remained, and he counted twelve people, including Fay. She might manage to convince more, but Mallory doubted her pack would have more than twenty members, if even that.

"This is your decision Fay," Kieran said. "Stay or go."

Fay stared at him for a second. Her expression relaxed, but it didn't last long. When it shuttered again, she turned around without saying anything. She walked away, and the people behind her followed.

Mallory and the others stayed where they were until everyone had vanished. The tension was still high, at least until Alpin broke it.

"Well, this was an exciting first hour being here. I wonder what's next?" he asked out loud.

A few people chuckled, and the tension vanished. Baxter and Robin made their way to their boyfriends while the others headed back inside. Mallory was sorry for Sloan and Kieran. They'd lost their father not so long ago, when Kieran had needed to take his father's place as the alpha, and now, they were losing their sister. It couldn't be easy for them to deal with this, even though, from what Mallory understood, the four of them never had a good relationship. But the safety of the pack was more important than their sister. It was one of the reasons Mallory knew they were good leaders. They'd had to choose, and even though the right decision had been the hardest one, it was the one they'd chosen.

"Is every evening so eventful?" Tynan asked as he and Mallory stepped into the house.

"Not this much, but there *have* been a lot of things happening. It's why I called you."

Tynan nodded. Like always, he was wearing dress pants and a shirt, along with a jacket. The style of his clothes had changed over the decades, but he still looked as distinguished and elegant as he'd been the night Mallory had met him. People saw him, and they didn't think he was dangerous because of the way he appeared. Nothing could be more different from the truth. Tynan was deadly to the people who threatened his family, and through Mallory, Arlen was now part of Tynan's family.

The dragon clan wouldn't know what hit it, and Mallory couldn't wait to see what would happen.

"Leave me the fuck alone," Merrick snapped from somewhere deeper in the house. Someone laughed, and Mallory would have recognized Alpin's laughter anywhere.

Not everyone might survive the fight, although it wouldn't be the dragon clan who killed Alpin.

It might just be Merrick.

"I apologize for the scene you had to witness," Kieran said as he walked into the living room, where everyone had gathered.

To Arlen's surprise, it was Tynan who got to his feet to meet him.

"Don't apologize for something you had no power over."

Kieran rubbed his face. "I don't know about that. There's probably something I should have done differently, but at the moment, I'm trying to keep the pack safe, and unfortunately, my sister doesn't understand that."

That gave Arlen pause. "She's your sister?" he blurted out.

Kieran nodded. He looked tired, but he was probably used to spending most of his time awake during the day. It couldn't be easy for him and Robin to make things work between them, and having so many vampires around didn't make it any easier.

"Yes," Sloan said. He walked in right after Kieran, and he looked just as tired. "Kieran and I were always closer, maybe because there was less age difference between us, or maybe because of the way our father treated us. Fay was the apple of his eyes, while Kieran could never do anything the way our father wanted. I was stuck in the middle, but I always felt closer to my brother than to my sister."

"And when I decided that the pack had gone through enough and that our father needed to step down as the alpha, Sloan supported me, while Fay supported our father," Kieran continued. "Our father has always been a bigot, a racist, and a homophobe. He hates anyone who isn't part of the pack, including other wolf shifters. He'd been starting fights with other packs, and I couldn't allow that to continue. But it was Robin who gave me the final push. I knew my father would never accept him, and I had to choose between the two of them." Kieran looked at Robin, who wrapped an arm around his waist. "I chose the right person."

"But your sister might not have been wrong," Rex said. Or at least, Arlen thought it was Rex. He wasn't quite sure who was who in Mallory's family yet, apart from Tynan.

"What do you mean?" Sloan asked.

"About the pack allying with the clan. From what little Mallory told us, the clan has been targeting vampires. Wouldn't it have been easier to ally with them?"

"Possibly, but there are several problems with that," Kieran said as he guided Robin toward one of the couches. "One of them is that both Sloan and I are dating vampires. That alone is enough for us not to want anything to do with the clan. The other is that it wouldn't be right. I truly believe vampires and wolves can live together in harmony. I'm not saying it will be easy, but the people in this room are proof of that. I don't want anyone else dying from this drug or any other drug. If I have to fight the clan to accomplish that, then I will. They're planning on fighting us, anyway. They want full control over our town, and it's not something I can accept."

"Which is why we're here," Tynan said. "We'll be more than happy to fight by your side."

Kieran bowed his head lightly. "Thank you. I do wonder why, though."

"It's not hard to understand. As you said, I believe vampires and wolves can live together. You and your vampire partners seem happy, and I want to see more of that. Beyond that, I agree with you that the clan needs to be stopped. Right now, they want control of the town, but what will they do once they have it? From what I know about them, I suspect they want to expand. They think a lot of themselves, and a victory, especially *this* victory, would only make them bolder."

"I suppose you're not wrong," Kieran said. He rubbed his jaw as he thought. "I'll need to ask the pack members if anyone wants to help, though I suspect that most will want to stay out of the fight. I don't blame them, but I know I can't."

"We'll need more allies," Tynan said.

That was where Arlen and Merrick came in. Arlen cleared his throat, and everyone looked at him. He wasn't used to being the center of attention, so he focused on Tynan. "As I already told Mallory and his team, I think Merrick and I can help with that. When we left the clan, we decided we needed to make friends with the supernatural community in town. They needed to see that we weren't a threat and that we were nothing like the clan. We made friends with several people, including satyrs, witches, and other creatures who could be useful. We've been contacting everyone we can think of and explaining to them what's happening. We've already convinced several groups to help, but we're not done yet."

Tynan smiled.

That made Arlen feel proud, which didn't make sense. He just wanted to please Mallory's family so they would accept him as Mallory's partner.

"What do we do in the meantime? Actually, what do we do, period? Will we attack the clan, or will we have to wait until they take the first step?" Tynan asked.

Arlen wasn't sure how to answer that question. "They won't attack us up front, but they'll be ready if we do. We know where the clan lives and how many dragons live there, but we're going to have to be smart about this. We'll need to take the dragons down one by one, unfortunately. It would be too easy for them to shift and take us down if we attack. Merrick and I would be able to fight them in their dragon form, but I don't think any of you could. You might be able to do so in a team, but we need more people."

"So that's it?" Alpin asked, looking around the room. "We wait?"

"Patience is a virtue you still have to learn," Tynan told him.

Alpin pouted. "Waiting is boring." His gaze stopped on Merrick, and he grinned, exposing his fangs. "Or maybe not.

I'm sure I can find something to do in the meantime. Or maybe someone."

Arlen had to admire his stubbornness, and honestly, he wasn't sure who would win this fight of wills between him and Merrick. Merrick could out-stubborn anyone, but Arlen suspected he'd met his match.

Maybe the wait wouldn't be as boring as everyone expected.

"I've never had sex with a dragon shifter," Alpin continued. He was bouncing in his armchair by now.

"And you never will," Merrick said with a growl.

Alpin cocked his head. "How do you know? You're not the only dragon shifter available in town."

"No, but all the others belong to the clan, except for Arlen. They'd rather kill you than touch you in any way."

Alpin wiggled his eyebrows. "I'm persuasive."

"And they're deadly," Merrick snapped. "Don't be an id-iot—or, be an idiot and see what happens. I don't care."

Alpin glared at him. "I think you do care. You wouldn't be all growly if you didn't." His expression smoothed out. "You're awfully protective, and that's hot. Do that growl thing again?"

Merrick shot to his feet. Arlen moved, hoping to reach him in time to stop him from strangling Alpin or maybe tear out his fangs, but Merrick didn't move toward the vampire. Instead, he turned around and stomped out of the room, still muttering to himself.

"Did you really have to push him?" Tynan asked. He pinched the bridge of his nose as if he was exhausted from having to deal with Alpin's antics. He probably was. If this was what it was like regularly, Arlen could understand.

"But it's fun," Alpin said. "And you just said we wouldn't be having any fun until we take out a good number of drag-ons."

"Merrick isn't one of the dragons we have to take out. We need him, so try not to push him into fleeing, all right?"

Alpin pouted again. When he did that, he looked even more like an angel, but Arlen was starting to realize he was anything but.

"Fine. I'll stay away from Merrick, at least for now. But since we're talking about taking out the dragons one by one, we need to come up with a strategy. I can think of a few."

One of Alpin's brothers interrupted him, but Arlen wasn't listening to them bickering anymore. He was worried about Merrick, but not because of anything Alpin had done or said. Merrick had always had a short temper, but it was even worse these days. Hopefully, he'd reacted so strongly because Alpin had been the one teasing him, but Arlen would have to talk to him. He could deal with losing his apartment, his car, and the club.

But he couldn't deal with losing Merrick.

Chapter Six

Nothing was happening. Mallory was used to this kind of thing when he and the others were on missions, but he couldn't say it felt good. Just like everyone else, he wanted to do something, stop the dragons from selling deadly drugs and taking over the town, but there was nothing they could do.

Alpin's plan of going into town and seducing the first dragon he could find was starting to sound good.

Mallory sighed and thumped the back of his head against the wall. He was on the porch swing, staring out at the forest, overthinking this entire thing. Before they did anything, they had to allow Kieran, Merrick, and Arlen to contact more allies. The more people were on their side, the better chance they had to be successful against the dragons.

Besides, there were plenty of things to do around pack territory. Fay and a dozen other people had left the pack, abandoning their homes and even their families in some cases. Mallory had no idea where they'd gone, but if he had to bet, he'd say they'd see them again. Fay clearly had a grudge against her brothers, and Mallory doubted she'd let it go, especially since her father had left with her. Mallory had only seen him from a distance, but he'd easily heard him, so he knew how much of an asshole the guy was. He didn't deserve two sons like Sloan and Kieran, who were doing everything they could to protect the pack, the people they loved, and their town.

"What are you doing here?" Arlen asked.

Mallory turned to see him leaning against the doorframe, his arms crossed over his chest. Like always, he was beautiful. His dark hair was swept away from his face, and his cheeks were flushed. More than that, Mallory knew he was beautiful inside. He'd watched the way Arlen treated his siblings, the way they'd interacted, and he could see that Arlen would fit right in. He couldn't have been happier. He wouldn't have let go of Arlen even if his family had hated him, but this would make things easier.

"Just thinking," Mallory told him as he patted the spot next to him on the swing.

But Arlen shook his head. "I have something to do tonight."

"Yeah? Can I ask what it is?"

Arlen's smile was easy and beautiful. "Always. I want to go to the club."

He and Merrick had stayed away from it until now. Mallory knew they were dealing with the cleanup and insurance, but from a distance. It had to hurt to see all their work and their home burned to the ground.

Mallory got to his feet. "How come? You need something from there?"

"No, and even if I did, I doubt whatever I needed would have survived. I want to see what's left."

"And then?" Mallory had been wondering for a while now. He hadn't wanted to bring it up because he didn't want to hurt Arlen by reminding him of the club, but maybe it was time.

"And then, I'll rebuild. Well, Merrick and I will. He's always been a partner, even though he was a silent one."

"So he's on board with this?"

"Yes."

"What about the clan? Will they try to stop you?"

Arlen's smile turned feral. "I mentioned that to Merrick,

and his answer mirrored my thoughts."

"I'm almost afraid to ask what his answer was."

Arlen laughed. "He said, and I quote, *fuck them*."

"I have to agree."

"So you believe we should rebuild, too?"

"I believe you should do whatever you want. I won't deny I'm afraid of what would happen if the clan attacked again, but I know they'll find and hurt you anywhere you are if that's what they want. Keeping you in pack territory won't help in the end, and we can't hide for the rest of eternity."

Arlen hooked an arm around Mallory's shoulders and pulled him close. "Sometimes, it's tempting to do just that. I could keep you to myself, and we wouldn't have to deal with any of this."

"But you'd hate yourself. The club is important to you, but it's not the only thing. You want everyone in town to be safe, and that will only happen if we deal with the clan."

But Mallory couldn't help but wonder how Merrick and Arlen would feel about that. From what he'd gathered, they'd left the clan because they'd had to. While Mallory understood and agreed with their decision, the clan was still their family, or rather, it had been for a long time. It couldn't be easy for them to fight against the clan, just like it wouldn't be easy for Mallory to fight against his family. If he had to, if one of his siblings or his father did something so horrible that he couldn't avoid stepping in, he would, but his heart would break.

Arlen kissed Mallory's temple. "So, I was wondering if you wanted to come with me," he said.

"To the club?"

"Yes. I realize there's probably nothing I can do there, but I still want to see what the clan did to Merrick and me."

Mallory looked up at him. "About that. Do you think you'll be able to fight them? They're your family."

Arlen shook his head. "They never were a true family, not like you and your siblings. The clan isn't like the pack, either. I think that it comes from the fact that dragons never lived in clans before. We're solitary creatures, and when we do live with someone, it's a partner or a best friend."

"Like you and Merrick."

"Exactly. As things evolved and time passed, we realized it would be safer for us to be in clans, but we never came to care for each other the way you and your siblings do or how the pack members care about each other. It's just a bunch of people living together who share the same quirk of being able to turn into a dragon."

Mallory found himself grinning. "I wouldn't call it a quirk."

"Whatever you want to call it, it doesn't change the fact that the clan was never my family. Merrick is. *You* are, and I guess that in a way, the pack is, too. I hope that even when this is over and we can all go back to our lives, the pack will stay an ally, and possibly a friend. I like Kieran and Sloan and their boyfriends."

"Should I be jealous?"

"Never." Arlen leaned down and kissed Mallory on the lips this time. "So? Are we going?"

Mallory had better ideas about what they could do with their night, but he could tell this was important to Arlen and wanted to give him everything he needed. So he nodded. "We can go now, unless you have something else to do."

"No. I was just looking for you to ask if you wanted to come along."

It took them fifteen minutes to finally get out of the front door. People kept stopping them, and mostly, those people belonged to Mallory's family. In the end, he grabbed Arlen's hand, dragged him away while ignoring the fact that Meyer was trying to talk to him, and slammed the door in Meyer's face.

Arlen was still laughing as they got to his car. "I love your family," he said.

"Most of the time, I love them, too, but they can be a lot."

"Maybe so, but having so many people who care about you and who you care about is a miracle."

Arlen's voice had gone wistful, and Mallory pulled him close and kissed him again. "Well, they're all yours now. You can run, but you can't hide from them, especially Alpin. We'll find you even if you try to leave us behind."

Arlen buried his hand into Mallory's hair. "Why would I want that? You've given me everything I've ever wanted and things I never knew I wanted. Unless you tell me to go, I'm never leaving you, Mallory."

Mallory's heart raced. "The same goes for me. As far as I'm concerned, we can spend the rest of eternity together."

"And we will."

As soon as they dealt with the clan, anyway.

Even though Arlen hadn't seen the club since the night of the fire, he knew what to expect. Merrick had come around to make sure everything was secure and start making a list of the things they needed to do, and he'd warned Arlen.

It still hurt to see the blackened ruins that were the only things left from the place he'd poured so much of himself into. He'd rebuild, but that didn't lessen the pain, although it was mixed with the fierce anger and resolution to make the clan pay. They'd thought they would win this fight, but one way or another, Arlen would make sure they didn't.

"You okay?" Mallory asked from beside Arlen.

Arlen found himself smiling, even though there was little to smile about. "I've been better, but I'm fine."

"It's pretty bad."

It was. Two walls were still standing, but the other two had collapsed. There was no ceiling anymore, and everything inside was gone, from the tables to the chairs to the bar counters. The upper floor was only a memory, which meant that the apartment where Merrick and Arlen had lived was, too. They'd lost everything, and while the pack had been good enough to let them stay with them, Arlen couldn't help but wonder if it would be forever. It was probably better for them to stay there until the clan was dealt with, but how long would that take?

Arlen was in no rush to leave the pack. Staying with them meant he was staying with Mallory, and he was more than happy to. Mallory had been talking about forever with him, and that was what Arlen wanted, but Arlen had questions about that.

"What will you do once the clan is dealt with?" he asked.

Mallory blinked. "That's an odd turn of the conversation."

"I was just thinking that Merrick and I are lucky the pack welcomed us and that I don't want to be anywhere else because it means I'm with you, but what about when the clan is dealt with and you leave?"

"We were just telling each other that this was forever. Why do you think I'm going anywhere?"

Arlen supposed he was right. They *had* been telling each other they'd be together forever, and Arlen hoped that would happen. "Well, you're a conclave enforcer. I know you're on a sabbatical, but eventually, you'll have to go back to work."

"Not if I leave the conclave."

Arlen sucked in a breath and turned his attention fully on Mallory. Who cared about the club? Mallory was more important. "What are you talking about?"

"Just that I'd been thinking about leaving the conclave even before meeting you."

"Why?"

"It's a mix of things. The team was a family, but Baxter and Robin left, and the conclave didn't want our team to help them. I don't want to lose two of the people I consider my brothers, plus I dislike the fact that the conclave only wants the safety of the people they say should be protected. It's not fair, and I'm not even talking about other supernatural creatures. Baxter and Robin are in danger, yet the conclave ordered us to leave."

"But you didn't."

Mallory shook his head. "We couldn't. What would happen to them if we left? We can't risk it, and I can't help but wonder what the conclave will think once this is over. They won't be happy about the fact that we took things in hand and dealt with the clan. They'll also be pissed that we worked with other supernatural creatures, especially wolves."

Arlen tsked. "I never understood this animosity between vampires and wolves. I mean, it's obvious the two can work together, and pretty well. You just have to watch your friends with their boyfriends."

"It's from a long time ago, but you're right. Wolves are people, just like vampires, and that's how we should behave instead of trying to kill each other." Mallory looked out at the club again. "So, what are we doing here?"

Arlen looked out at the club, too. "Honestly, I'm not sure. I didn't have to come, but I wanted to see what the clan has done."

"Unless I'm wrong, I'm pretty sure they're about to do something else," Mallory said.

Arlen frowned and looked up in the direction where Mallory was looking. He swore when he saw two men striding down the sidewalk, coming toward them. He recognized them as clan members, so Mallory was right. "They've come to gloat," he said.

"Why am I not surprised?" Mallory muttered.

"Because even though you don't know the clan, you're a good judge of character."

"I don't know about that. They make it easy to understand they're assholes. Will they attack us?"

"It's a possibility." Arlen looked around. It was the middle of the night, and the area had been pretty empty before he opened the club. With the club burned down, it was quiet again. A few people were around, but they were rushing down the sidewalk, clearly on their way somewhere. Hopefully, they wouldn't notice whatever was about to happen, although Arlen wouldn't bet on it. The clan always enjoyed making a mess, and he doubted this time would be any different.

He recognized the dragons from the last time they'd been here. Warner looked uncomfortable, and he kept peering around as if he expected someone to attack. Clement, on the other hand, was positively gleeful.

"You knew what would happen if you went against the clan," he declared when he and Warner reached Mallory and Arlen.

Mallory took a step forward, but Arlen put a hand on his shoulder to keep him back. "What do you want?" he asked.

"I wanted to see that you aren't so smug anymore. You lost everything."

And Clement was clearly happy about that. He was smirking, trying to goad Arlen, and he might have managed if Arlen hadn't known that was what he was doing. Arlen had no intention of being the one to attack first.

"If you're here because the clan sent you, you can go back and tell them that Merrick and I will rebuild. We won't let this stop us."

"The clan won't allow you to do that." Clement took a step forward.

Warner followed quickly and almost stumbled. Clement

shot him a disgusted look, which made Warner cringe back.

"I don't care what the clan will or won't allow me to do. I'm not a clan member, and I'll do whatever I want," Arlen told him.

"Then we'll have to intervene."

Clement telegraphed what he was about to do way before he did. Arlen had all the time in the world to move away from the punch aimed at his face. Clement looked pissed that he didn't hit Arlen, and he roared, the sound echoing off the ruins of the club.

Then Clement started shifting.

Arlen swore and looked around, but even though a few people were still on the sidewalks, he couldn't avoid shifting. He couldn't fight Clement in his human form.

The problem was that there were two dragons. Warner was shifting, too, and there was no way Arlen could fight two adult dragons.

"Take care of Clement," Mallory said. He cracked his knuckles. "I'll take care of this one."

"He's a dragon shifter," Arlen said rather stupidly.

Mallory grinned at him. "I've always wanted to fight a dragon. I just need to avoid the claws, the fangs, the tail, and everything else, right?"

Arlen prayed Mallory wouldn't get hurt, but they didn't have a choice. He just had to hope that Mallory could deal with Warner, but just in case, he'd have to get rid of Clement as soon as possible.

He shifted, too, mourning the loss of his shirt. Since he'd bought it, it had become a favorite of his, but he supposed he could always go back to the store and get a new one. He should know better than to wear his favorite clothes when there was a possibility the clan would attack.

Arlen turned to Clement.

The other dragon was smaller than him, and there was no

doubt in Arlen's mind that he was also younger. Arlen wasn't surprised to find out he was impulsive. Clement threw himself at him without waiting for Arlen to shift, but Arlen had expected it. He ducked out of the way, then shook out his wings, expanding them. It would be better if he managed to intimidate Clement into stopping this madness.

It didn't work. Arlen hadn't expected it to, but he would have felt better if Clement hadn't been an idiot. As it was, Arlen could already see a few people had stopped walking and were staring up at them, gaping. One of them had his phone in his hand, which meant the existence of dragon shifters wouldn't be a secret for much longer.

Arlen didn't care. He wouldn't be the one to deal with the consequences, and it wasn't his fault. The clan had started this, and if anyone had a problem with what was happening, they could take it up with them.

Mallory had never fought a dragon shifter, but there was a first time for everything. He was pretty sure he wouldn't enjoy the experience, but he was ready to kick scaly ass, and from the looks of things, he'd have the opportunity tonight.

Arlen was already fighting with the other dragon, so Mallory focused on the one in front of him. The man had shifted, but he seemed less enthusiastic than his friend about turning Mallory into a burned pancake.

Mallory walked around Warner. Warner thumped his tail on the ground, making everything around Mallory shake. He reached for Mallory, but Mallory quickly danced out of the way. Warner followed, but he looked almost like he didn't want to do this. He was slow, not putting much energy into the fight, and when Mallory turned around and punched him, he stumbled back as if Mallory had way more force than he did. Mallory was a vampire, and he trained to be able to fight pretty much anything, but no vampire could be as strong as a dragon. Yet Warner was acting as if Mallory had hurt him.

That gave Mallory pause. Why would Warner do something like that? Mallory remembered him from the fight at the club, but even then, Warner had been a follower, not the one who'd started the fight. It was clear that Clement was the leader of the two. Warner didn't look like he wanted to be here, and Mallory could take advantage of that.

Once Warner was done acting as if Mallory had torn off one of his wings and chewed on it, Mallory rushed forward. Warner made a strange squeak, but he allowed Mallory to wrap an arm around his neck. Mallory pressed his back against Warner's shoulder, but he didn't put too much force into his arm. He didn't want to strangle Warner, even though he could do it in this position. He just acted as if that was what he was trying to do, and as he did so, he leaned closer.

"You don't want to fight me," he murmured.

Warner tried to pull away, but he didn't put much force into it. Then he quickly shook his head. He was a pretty good actor. Mallory had to give him that, because he suspected no one would know they weren't really fighting from the outside. He was even sweating, for fuck's sake. It took a lot of force to keep Warner where he was, and Warner wasn't even really trying to get away. Mallory could only imagine what would happen if he was.

"You don't have to stay with the clan," Mallory quickly added. "I know it's scary, but you can join us at the pack. We won't push you away if you come."

Warner's eyes widened, and he shook his head again. This time, when he pushed away from Mallory, he put more force into it, and Mallory had to let him go. He stayed close, grabbing one of Warner's wings and holding on.

"We won't let the clan hurt you," he promised. "You can even help us make sure the clan doesn't hurt anyone else ever again."

But Warner wasn't listening, or at least Mallory didn't think he was. Warner raised his wing and wiggled it, and Mallory had to let go. He dropped to the ground and rolled, then quickly got back to his feet and risked a glance at Arlen and Clement.

Arlen had Clement on the ground. Clement was on his back, his wings spread by his sides. He was trying to get back to his feet, but Arlen had a paw pressed to his throat. It was clear that he wouldn't hesitate to hurt Clement.

Clement hesitated, then snarled and looked around. His gaze stopped on Warner, who seemed frozen. Mallory had no idea what was happening in Warner's mind, but since he didn't seem to want to leave the clan, they needed to at least act as if they were fighting. So Mallory quickly twisted around and aimed a punch at Warner's nose.

Warner stumbled forward, reaching for his nose with one of his paws. He made a wounded sound, as if Mallory had betrayed him, and Mallory supposed he had. They hadn't talked about it, but it was clear that Warner wanted nothing to do with what was happening and that Mallory was letting him get away with it.

It didn't look like Clement would. He roared, and Warner threw himself forward, scrambling to help him. Mallory ran after him and jumped onto his back, clinging to the spikes. His body kept slipping to the side, but he couldn't put himself in the middle of Warner's back, not unless he wanted to be skewered by the spikes.

Warner twisted his neck and caught Mallory's jeans. He pulled him down and threw him to the ground, hard enough that the air whooshed out of Mallory's lungs.

Arlen roared and let go of Clement. He rushed toward Mallory, but Mallory was already getting to his feet and waving him away.

But it was too late. Clement was on his feet with his wings extended wide. He spat fire at Arlen, and while he couldn't burn down anything else, Mallory was close enough to Arlen that the fire would hit him, too. He winced, doubting a vampire could survive that kind of crispness, but the world turned black.

Arlen had wrapped his wings around him, protecting him from the fire. Mallory could still see its light and feel its warmth beyond the thin skin of Arlen's wings, so he could tell it didn't last long. As soon as the fire stopped, Arlen dropped his wings and shifted back.

When he peeked around Arlen to see that Clement and Warner were gone, Mallory understood why. When he looked up, he realized they were flying away. There were half a dozen people on the sidewalk, all of them with their phones out. Luckily, they were focused on the two dragons flying away and not on Arlen, who finished shifting and rushed toward his car. Mallory went after him, quickly ushering him into the backseat. By the time the people who'd been filming Clement and Warner were done and looking around for Arlen, there were no signs of him.

Mallory quickly grabbed the backpack he knew contained a change of clothes from the trunk, then walked around the car and hopped into the driver seat. He paused, realizing he didn't have the keys, but Arlen's hand appeared between the seats, the keys dangling from her finger.

"Weren't they in your jeans?" Mallory asked as he took them.

"I remembered to pick them up on my way back to the car."

"Good thinking."

Mallory turned on the engine and drove away from the club. There were still people standing on the sidewalk, talking excitedly to each other, and while he knew this was going to be a problem, he didn't care. What happened to the clan wasn't his problem, and as long as Arlen and Merrick stayed out of trouble, every human in the world could know about dragon shifters, as far as he was concerned.

"That could have gone better," he said.

Arlen sighed heavily. "I wish they hadn't shifted. It was a stupid thing to do, but I didn't expect anything different from Clement."

"Yeah, he doesn't look like the brightest bulb in the box."

"You fought Warner," Arlen continued.

Mallory shrugged. "I can't say he tried very hard. I wouldn't have been able to do half the things I did if he had been."

"What do you mean?"

"That I don't think Warner wanted to be here tonight and that I doubt he wants to fight the pack. He could have hurt me several times, possibly even killed me, but instead, he half-assed the fight. I managed to talk to him when I grabbed his neck, and I told him that he didn't have to do any of this if he didn't want to and that he could leave the clan and come to us."

Arlen squeezed Mallory's shoulder. "It's good that he didn't try to fight. No offense, but you wouldn't have been able to do much."

Mallory snorted. "I'm not offended by the truth. I might be trained, but I'm still only one vampire."

"Do you think he'll leave the clan?"

"I have no idea." Arlen knew these guys better than Mallory, but even he didn't know them well. "I hope so. You and Merrick left the clan because you disagreed with what the leader was doing. Surely you're not the only people who feel that way. I don't think many people will leave, but even if only a few agree to fight on our side, things will be easier for us." And there would be fewer chances that someone would get hurt, which was the most important thing as far as Mallory was concerned. He couldn't lose anyone from his family, be it Tynan and his siblings or the team.

And now, Arlen and Merrick.

They stayed silent on their way back to pack territory. Arlen continued thinking about what Mallory had said about Warner. He tried to remember as many things as he could about the other dragon, but there wasn't much in his memory. He barely knew Warner. He barely knew anyone from the clan except for Merrick. Dragons weren't made to live in clans, and the only reason they did was that there was safety in numbers. The clan needed that even more now that humans had found out about them.

That had been utterly stupid. Gerald would have Clement and Warner's asses once they were back with the clan, and it wouldn't be in a nice way. Maybe that would be the push Warner needed to leave the clan, maybe not. Arlen didn't know what to think of Warner, and he didn't care right now. He didn't want to think about the other dragon. He wanted only to think about Mallory and how he could have lost him so easily tonight.

If Warner hadn't been doubting the clan and what he and Clement were doing, he could have easily killed Mallory. The thought was enough to make Arlen shudder in horror, especially because there wouldn't have been anything he could do. He'd been fighting Clement, and unlike to Warner, Clement hadn't been pulling back his punches. Arlen had won the fight because he was older, more experienced, and bigger. He suspected he now had a mortal enemy in Clement, and while he didn't care, he couldn't help but wonder how it would change things for him. Gerald and Virginia were already aiming for him. Clement might hinder them, but he might also help them.

"What do you think will happen to Clement and Warner when they get back to the clan?" Mallory asked.

Arlen kept his focus on the road in front of the car. He was relieved to see they were almost to pack territory already. He had no idea when that had happened, but this place felt like home and like it was safe, and he sorely needed that after the fight. "He won't kill them, if that's what you're asking," he answered.

"There are ways to hurt people without killing them."

Arlen grimaced. "And Gerald is fond of using those ways." Which was one of the many reasons Arlen and Merrick had left. "I wouldn't be surprised if we didn't see Warner and Clement anytime soon."

Mallory was silent for a moment. "He'll torture them?"

"Probably. At the very least, he'll lock them up to make sure they learned their lesson."

"They just outed dragons to the entire world. That's one hell of a lesson."

"They should have thought better about what they were doing." But then, thinking had never been Clement's forte.

"I don't care about Clement, but I think we could pull Warner to our side."

"I hope you're right, but at the moment, there's nothing we can do about either of them."

Mallory took one last turn, and the driveway that led to the house the two of them and the others shared appeared. Arlen held his breath until they reached the house and parked in front of it. Then he was out of the car and by the driver's door in seconds. He pulled it open, dragged Mallory out of it, and hauled him into his arms.

Mallory didn't argue, as if he understood why Arlen was reacting this way. Arlen knew Mallory was okay and that there wasn't even a scratch on him, but he still needed to reassure himself, and hugging him was the best way to make that happen.

Mallory squeezed Arlen's waist. "I'm fine," he promised.

"I know." Arlen buried his nose into Mallory's hair and took a deep breath. Mallory *was* fine, and he was in Arlen's arms. No matter what happened, no matter what would happen in the future, that was the most important thing.

The door of the house flew open. Arlen looked up to find Merrick standing on the porch with his arms crossed over his chest, glaring at him. "You were supposed to check out what was left of the club. How is it that every human on social media is screeching about dragons, dinosaurs, and aliens?"

Arlen blinked. "Aliens?"

Merrick sighed so loudly that Arlen could hear him from where he was. His shoulders slumped, and he gestured at Arlen and Mallory to come into the house. "You should probably see this."

The only thing Arlen wanted to do was drag Mallory into the room they shared and make sure there was nothing wrong with him by checking every inch of his body, but instead, he allowed Mallory to link their fingers together and pull him into the house.

They went straight to the living room, where everyone was scattered in front of the TV. They didn't seem to be watching it, though. Everyone was on their phone, and when Arlen peeked at the screens, he could see they were on social media.

"What the fuck happened?" Merrick snapped.

Arlen wasn't offended by his friend's tone. Merrick was worried, and this was how he showed it. "Mallory and I were at the club when Clement and Warner arrived," he explained. He had everyone's attention now.

Merrick groaned and hung his head. "This makes more sense now. They're idiots."

"I can't say I disagree. They shifted first, and I had to shift to defend myself and Mallory."

Merrick eyed Mallory up and down. "How did you fight a dragon and come out in one piece?"

"Warner wasn't fighting back," Mallory explained. "I don't think he's okay with what the clan is doing, but he's terrified. He wasn't even trying to fight me, and when I pinned him down, I told him that he could come here if he ever wanted to leave the clan."

"I'm not sure that was a good idea."

Mallory shrugged. "I don't know, but the clan already knows we're staying here and that this is pack territory. Maybe if we can pull at least a few dragons from the clan to our side, it'll be easier for us to win this fight."

"I can't say I disagree," Oren said from his spot on the couch. He was on his phone, too, but he looked up as he spoke to Mallory. "But there's no way for us to know if we can trust these dragons."

"We don't have to trust them. If they come, we have to use them against the clan."

Arlen agreed with both of them. He couldn't trust anyone from the clan, and having anyone join their side of the fight would mean keeping an eye on them, but they needed more people. The clan was powerful, and it would be ideal if they could get dragons away from it and on their side.

"So what's this about aliens?" Mallory asked.

"People posted videos and pictures, but they're all pretty dark, so you can't see what's going on in them," Oren told him. "In some of the videos, you can't even recognize that the shapes are dragons. You can see two massive things flying away, though, so people have been guessing what those things might be. So far, I've seen mentioned aliens and dinosaurs, along with dragons."

"Someone even thought they were small airplanes," Merrick said. His tone of voice told everyone what he thought of that guess.

"Well, I can't say I'm happy that the clan outed dragons to the world, but as long as Merrick and I are careful not to shift where we shouldn't, we'll be fine."

"Yes, because you've never had to shift in front of anyone who didn't know about dragon shifters. Wait, isn't that what just happened?" Merrick asked.

Arlen glared at him. "If we don't have a choice, we'll do it, but it would be better for us to stick to pack territory for now."

There was nothing either of them could do back at the club. It had been stupid to go and check it out, especially when Merrick had already done so. Arlen had felt driven to see how much damage the clan had done to his life, and now, he had.

The clan stood to ruin his life even more now that humans knew dragons existed. He and Merrick would have to be even more careful, but that was fine. Arlen had been careful for decades, way more than some of the other clan dragons. Besides, he had a good reason to be careful now. He needed to keep Mallory safe, and if doing so meant he never left pack territory, he'd learn to like it.

CHAPTER SEVEN

Nothing was happening. Mallory had been sure that now that Arlen and Merrick had stood up to the clan so openly, the clan would try to take them out. Arlen and Merrick had been careful to stay in pack territory, so Mallory wasn't too worried, but the fact that the clan wasn't doing anything was starting to weigh heavily on his mind. It didn't sound like them to stay away from a fight.

Maybe it was because of what had happened at the burned-down club. The humans were still trying to figure out what had happened at the club. Luckily, none of the videos and pictures the people on the sidewalks had been taking were clear, which meant that most of them had been dismissed as fake or showing something entirely different from dragons. A couple of those humans still insisted that they knew what they'd seen, but people weren't listening to them. That was good because it meant that even though dragons had been exposed, for now, most humans still didn't believe they existed. Arlen and Merrick were safe, which in the end, was all that mattered to Mallory.

Mallory knew the clan was planning something, and both Arlen and Merrick agreed. They were planning something, too. They and the pack had been reaching out to everyone they thought might want to help in their fight, and they had good results. Several members of the supernatural community had promised they'd help in this fight, so their numbers were growing. The odds were still against them since they were fighting dragon shifters, but the pack wasn't alone anymore. Dozens of people were ready to help, and while Mallory hadn't expected it because of how tense things usually were between different supernatural creatures, he was glad to have this opportunity to work with them.

He was convinced more than ever that even once this was over, he wouldn't go back to the conclave. He wanted to continue talking with people he normally wouldn't talk to. He didn't want to have to fight wolves or witches because that was what the conclave wanted him to do. It wasn't right.

"What are you doing out here?" a voice Mallory recognized all too well asked from behind him. "Playing the brooding hero? Where's your damsel in distress?"

Mallory narrowed his eyes at Alpin. "What do you want?"

"I was just checking on my big brother. Is that so bad?" He flopped onto the porch swing next to Mallory. "So? Where's your better half?"

"He and Merrick are working in the house."

They'd started rebuilding the club, and they'd decided to make it bigger and even better than the old one had been. Mallory wasn't sure how they were planning to do that, but it wasn't his area of expertise. They knew what they were doing, and lately, they'd been spending a lot of time on their computers and phones.

Luckily, that was all business they had to do during the day, which meant that the nights were dedicated to Mallory. Arlen's schedule had always leaned to nocturnal, so it wasn't a huge change for him to shift things so he and Mallory could spend time together. Even like this, they didn't see each other nearly enough some nights.

Mallory was still training, and the pack, Tynan, and Oren had decided to put together patrols. The clan was planning something, and even though no one knew what that something was, they expected the dragons to eventually attack. The pack needed to be protected when that happened, and

Mallory and the others had been pulled into the creation and training of pack security. There had been a few guards before, but there hadn't been nearly enough, and they hadn't been trained well. From what Kieran had said, his father had never made it a priority because he believed no one would dare attack the pack.

Mallory was pretty sure that the pack would be attacked, and soon. So they needed all the help and security they could get, including Mallory's family. Of course, Alpin wasn't a great help when it came to training others to fight, but he was a good distraction. Some pack members were terrified about what would happen and what the dragons would do, and he didn't blame them for that. They also disliked vampires, but if there was one person who might be able to make them change their mind, it was Alpin.

Alpin pushed the swing back, then kicked his feet up like a child when he let go. "You know, this wasn't what I expected when you called us for help," he said.

"No? What did you expect then?"

Alpin shrugged. "I didn't think you were involved with a dragon."

"I wasn't back then."

"Really? Because to me, it looks like you and Arlen have been together forever."

That made Mallory smile. "We haven't been."

"But he's it for you, right?"

"I'm pretty sure he is," Mallory agreed. He and Arlen had already promised forever to each other, and he intended to keep that promise, no matter what happened around them.

"How does it feel?" Alpin asked.

Mallory blinked, wondering what his brother was talking about for a moment. He was surprised when he realized that Alpin was asking how it felt to have someone like Arlen in his life, someone he loved so much that he was ready to sacrifice anything for him.

"This isn't like you," Mallory carefully said.

"What isn't like me?" Alpin was keeping his tone light, but Mallory could hear the warning in it.

"Well, you're not a one-guy kind of person."

"Why not? You don't think I could keep someone interested enough that they'd want to spend the rest of their life with me?"

"That's not what I said."

"It's what you implied."

"Do you blame me? Because for as long as I've known you, you've gone from bed to bed. No one seems to matter to you beyond what they can give you for one night."

"I don't see how that's a bad thing."

"I never said it was a bad thing. I'm surprised by what you are asking, that's all."

Alpin shrugged. "I guess I'm curious. I see how much Arlen matters to you and how much you're ready to sacrifice for him." Alpin hesitated. "You're going to leave the conclave, aren't you?"

Mallory wasn't surprised that his brother had realized that. Hopefully he was one of the few, since Mallory intended to keep it to himself for a while longer. He'd tell his team eventually, but for now, it was a secret he didn't want to burden them with. There would be plenty of time to talk things out once the fight with the dragons was over.

But no matter how flighty Alpin seemed, he'd always been good at reading other people, especially his siblings. Sometimes, it was annoying. Other times, like now, it made Mallory wonder how deep Alpin was. Alpin did his best to convince everyone that he was an idiot, but he really wasn't.

"I think I will," he confirmed. "But it's not because of Arlen, at least not entirely. I don't like the way the conclave has been going, and when they forbid us to help Baxter and

Robin, I knew I couldn't support them."

Alpin nodded. "It makes sense. I wouldn't be surprised if they lost your entire team. With all of you being on sabbatical, you'll eventually realize that the things you do for the conclave, you can do much better on your own or with your allies."

Maybe Alpin wasn't wrong. The team was already shifting things around, getting used to living away from the conclave. Darren and Caley had requested a sabbatical, too, as soon as they'd heard what was happening, and they'd join the rest of the team soon, along with Aubrey, Oren's boyfriend. Ignatius had gone back to the coven to be with Oscar and the child they'd adopted, and while Mallory was sad to have him so far away, he understood how important family was. He wouldn't be surprised if this gave Ignatius the push he needed to step away from the conclave permanently.

Alpin patted Mallory's knee and got to his feet. "Well, your boyfriend is coming downstairs. I can hear him from here. I guess the two of you need some time alone, so I'll skedaddle."

Mallory laughed. "You'll what?"

But Alpin was already gone. The door was open, and when Mallory turned, he could see Arlen coming down the stairs. He was talking on the phone, but when he noticed Mallory looking at him, he smiled, quickly said goodbye to whoever he'd been talking to, and hung up. Then he came outside to sit next to Mallory.

Mallory leaned against his side. Arlen wrapped an arm around Mallory's shoulders, and they sat together, in silence, watching the dark forest in front of the house.

They didn't need to say anything. They'd already told each other that they were in this for the long term, whatever it meant. Mallory didn't want to obsess over what it would be before the clan had been dealt with, but of one thing he was sure of when it came to his future, regardless of how long it would be.

He'd spend it with Arlen.

ABOUT THE AUTHOR

Catherine is the creator of several series, most of them paranormal, including the Whitedell Pride Series and the Gillham Pack Series. While she graduated in translation, she decided to go the writer's way because it was more fun to create her own stories and characters.

She's been living in Italy for more than twenty years, but she's a daughter of the North—Belgium to be precise—and she misses it so much that she's already planning to move back.

She loves pizza—probably too much—her son, her pets, and of course, books. She sneaks some reading time into her schedule every time she has five minutes free from writing, demands from her various pets and son, and lastly, housework.

Connect with her:

lievens.catherine@gmail.com
BookBub: https://www.bookbub.com/authors/catherine-lievens
Website: https://authorcatherinelievens.com/
Facebook: https://www.facebook.com/catherine.lievens.9
Facebook Group: https://www.facebook.com/groups/411788002341528/
Twitter: https://twitter.com/authorCLievens
Newsletter: http://eepurl.com/c-uvKn

www.ingramcontent.com/pod-product-compliance
Lightning Source LLC
Chambersburg PA
CBHW060634130626
46555CB00002B/803